HAVE YOURSELF A CHRISTIANSEN CHRISTMAS

A HOLIDAY STORY FROM YOUR FAVORITE SMALL TOWN FAMILY

SUSAN MAY WARREN

PRAISE FOR THE CHRISTIANSEN FAMILY SERIES

Have Yourself a Christiansen Christmas

The perfect return to one of my favorite families and fictional towns. This book couldn't have been more satisfying. Talk about a Susan May Warren character reunion! -Kelly, The Cozy Bookworm

Oh, how I love this family, the Christiansens. This series has been the absolute best in Christian fiction in my opinion! And Warren includes some mighty big spiritual truths, too. -Susan, Goodreads

I absolutely enjoyed diving back into this family and hearing about how their lives were going. It was like a reunion to "see" them all again. And now, I want a Christmas at Evergreen Resort! – Amy, Goodreads

Have Yourself a Christiansen Christmas brings back the entire Christiansen family in a heartwarming return to Deep Haven. This novella is such a beautiful tale of God's love for us and the perfect book for this holiday season. -Nicole, BookBub

Christiansen Family Series

Warren once again creates a compelling community full of vivid individuals whose anguish and dreams are so real and relatable, readers will long for every character to attain the freedom their hearts desire. -Booklist, *Take a Chance on Me*

Warren lays bare her characters' human frailties, including fear, grief, and resentment, as openly as she details their virtues of love, devotion, and resiliency. – Publishers Weekly, *Take a Chance on Me*

Warren has shaped a beautifully dynamic romance that teaches the value of family and forgiveness through a modern-day prodigal-son story of redemption. -Publishers Weekly, *You're the One That I Want*

ABOUT THE BOOK...

Please...come home for Christmas...

It's Christmas in the winter wonderland town of Deep Haven, and the Christiansen kids are all heading home for the holidays. But no one feels very merry.

- Grace is worried about her husband's life-changing illness...
- Eden is facing devastating news...
- Casper is in over his head (of course!)...
- Amelia is dodging a walk down the aisle...
- Owen...well, Owen just nearly died, again...
- But it's Darek who has news that just might destroy the family legacy.

The trip home for all is filled with secrets, memories and old dreams. But when they discover the real reason they've been asked home for the holidays, it will shake their world. It'll take a disaster for them to discover that home is the place for answers, hope and most of all...miracles.

This year, spend Christmas with your favorite small-town family

Soli Deo Gloria

My deepest gratitude goes to my amazing
Deep Haven girls:
Bobbi, Lisa, Rachel, Andrea & Michelle

And to the brilliant
Rel Mollet
I'd be a disaster without you!

PROLOGUE

Dear Children,

~~For a long time, we've needed to tell you...~~
~~Mom and I want to update you...~~
~~Everyone expects this, but no one wants to hear it...~~
~~It's important that we...~~
~~Please come home for Christmas...~~
~~Hope you are well. If you were to make it home for Christmas this year...~~
~~We love you. Hope you can make it home for Christmas.~~
Dear Children,
Hope you have a Merry Christmas.
Love,
Mom & Dad

1

It would be the perfect Christmas.

Grace should just calm down.

Inhale the peace that was her small northern town.

Because it was a beautiful, perfect Friday afternoon in the village on the lake where time lingered. Where fishing boats still motored out to the deep blue in the waxing dawn, and the locals spun tales over coffee and donuts at the Blue Loon cafe or quietly rustled through the pages of the community paper, filled with recipes and pictures of the recent performance of *The Worst Christmas Pageant Ever*.

Nothing to be scared about. Everyone was fine.

Especially since Max had put on skates today. Put on skates and announced he was joining in the community hockey game this afternoon.

In fact, he'd been happier than she'd seen him in months.

See, everything would be just fine.

If only, deep in her soul, she could escape this looming sense of doom.

As if the world was about to explode.

The fog hovered over the chilly, unbroken harbor of Deep

Haven, as if it too waited, its breath caught in the stillness of the crisp day. A tenacious and bold sun glimmered, casting through the haze, turning the horizon almost golden.

Fresh cedar boughs wrapped the lamp posts along Main Street, and twinkle lights edged the row of shops, from Java Cup down to World's Best Donuts in anticipation of the cheer that the forecast promised.

They'd had a rough start with an early season blizzard that had caused a few accidents, and then, as Minnesota weather would have it, a post-Thanksgiving heatwave that erased all the snow and turned the ground muddy.

But Deep Haven held its own magic for happy endings. The forecast called for a White Christmas and Grace half expected Bing Crosby and Danny Kaye to show up with Rosemary Clooney for a merry soft shoe in Bear Tree Park.

Yes, she had a perfect day in her perfect life. The one Grace had crafted with her former hockey-star husband, Max, and their adopted daughter, Yulia.

And right now, Grace should just embrace this perfect moment, with a perfect cup of coffee — a Vivien, a local favorite — as she climbed the bleacher steps of the outdoor hockey rink. She waved to Annalise Decker, her friend Colleen's mom, and—look at that—Noelle and Eli Hueston were back from Florida, all bundled up around their tanned faces.

"Welcome back," she said to them.

"Hi, Grace," Noelle said. "Tell your mother I'll give her a call soon to catch up."

"I will." Grace sat down behind them next to her thirteen-year-old daughter. Yulia wore a stocking cap, her tawny brown hair long down her back, a pair of jeans, Uggs, and a green ski jacket, her breath caught in crystalline puffs as she stared at her phone.

"Hey," Grace said. "I brought you a hot cocoa."

"Thanks." Yulia looked up and gave her a smile. "Dad made a goal."

Grace shot a look out to the ice rink where a number of the local guys she recognized—Peter and Nick Dahlquist, Sheriff Kyle Hueston and his brother Kirby, as well as pastor Dan Matthews and her brother Darek and his son Tiger—played a game of rink hockey. No pads, no checking, just a group of locals, and some weekenders, who loved to slap around a puck for fun.

Her guy—former right winger for the Minnesota Blue Ox professional hockey team Max Sharpe—was having a good week—no, a good *year*. Between the cocktail of drugs, healthy eating, and a toxin-free house, he'd found his old verve just two weeks ago, right after the town had re-flooded the rink. Grace had found him sharpening his skates and re-taping his hockey stick.

And humming.

Yes, her champion husband was back, and she relished every precious moment.

Now, he was showing off. Not as fast as he once was, he still handled the puck like it was glued to him, every bit a talent on the ice as Grace was with food.

Especially when he stole it from a big man she didn't know.

"C'mon, Ham, don't give it up so easily!" The shout came from a blonde sitting a row down and over from Grace. Next to her sat her daughter, probably, also with blonde hair, about the same age as Yulia. And next to her, a petite woman with long dark hair.

"Jake! Get in there!" the brunette yelled.

On the ice, a man went after Max, and Grace braced herself. Hockey, by nature, was a violent sport and —

Don't check him! She wanted to shout it, but that would only make Max seem like he needed protecting, and that was the last thing her brave, iron-tough husband needed.

Even if, with everything inside her, Grace longed to protect him, just a little longer.

But Max passed it off to her brother Darek and spun away from the oncoming rush. Wow, he was good, his moves solid and smooth on the ice.

"Are our guys winning?" Ivy, Darek's wife, slid on the row next to them, along with seven-year-old Joy. Her son, Tiger, was old enough to play this year and held his own on the ice with his father.

"Yes," Yulia said without looking up.

So she *was* paying attention, even while watching TikTok. Sometimes Grace wanted to take her phone and throw it into Lake Superior. It seemed the older Yulia got, the less she let them into her thoughts, her life.

In truth, Yulia had slowly slipped into the shadows since her thirteenth birthday last year. Of course, they'd had a lot to deal with—Max's first real symptoms had shown up around her birthday, and they'd spent that weekend down at the Mayo Clinic, bracing themselves for the prognosis.

Huntington's disease took no prisoners, but so far, they'd dodged its grip.

In her heart, she hoped they'd come up with some miraculous cure for the genetic disease and they'd dodge it forever.

Darek passed the puck off to Tiger, who slapped it at the goal.

Peter Dahlquist caught it in his glove—he was garbed up at least—and tossed it back out into the fray.

"Way to go, honey!" Ronnie Morales, his girlfriend and local paramedic shouted.

Peter raised his blocking glove to wave. Across the rink, Ronnie's brother, Tiago, stood with Josh Carter, who was watching his stepfather, Cole, scoop it up.

"Where's Casper?" Ivy asked as she blew on her own coffee. "He loves Saturday pickup games."

"I don't know. He missed last week too," Grace said. "Must be busy at the outfitter's shop. Christmas rush."

"For a millionaire, the guy puts in too many hours working."

"That's Casper. And all my brothers—they like to get in a good day's work. Apparently, they're not the only ones. Darek said you'd been extra busy at work."

Silence next to her made Grace turn.

Ivy was twirling her daughter's ultra-blonde hair out of her hat.

"For a lawyer, you don't have much of a poker face."

Ivy sighed. "I've been appointed to a judgeship."

The opposing team took that moment to charge down the ice, Nick with the puck. He flicked it at Pastor Dan, at goal. He gloved it easily.

Grace turned back to Ivy. "That's fantastic. We could use a good judge in Deep Haven."

Ivy made a face. "It's not in Deep Haven. It's in Duluth. It's just a temporary appointment—I'm filling in for a judge who passed away. Just a year left on his term, but..."

Dan shot the puck out and Kyle picked it up and slapped it deep toward the other side.

Darek nabbed it.

"You're thinking of taking it," Grace said.

Darek passed it off to Tiger. He was immediately pounced on by Kirby but managed to shoot it away.

Max picked it up.

"So you'll commute?" Grace asked, eyes on the game.

"No," Ivy said, and it was the tone in her voice that made Grace turn, meet her eyes. "We'll move."

It took a second for the words to sink in. Move? "What about the resort? Darek runs it...and..."

"I know. But it's just for a year. Maybe your dad can take over. Or...Max could help?"

Max? Oh, well...yes, maybe. He'd been restless lately, his

days usually filled with lifting weights and working out, helping the local high school coach, and his PR work for the Huntington's foundation. Since the fresh prognosis almost a year ago, he'd become more withdrawn, but getting out, like he was today, would do him good—

"Yeah, maybe that could—"

"Mom!"

Yulia hit her feet. "Mom! Dad's *hurt!*"

Grace's eyes found him on the ice where he'd fallen, where his body was jerking in a full-out seizure.

Grace didn't remember leaving the stands or even sliding out onto the ice, but in a moment, she'd hit her knees at his side. Kyle had reached him first and shoved a shirt under his head to keep him from hitting it on the ice. A couple guys had turned him onto his side. But he'd clearly bit his tongue because blood trickled out of his mouth.

"Max!" Grace reached for him but a voice behind her stopped her.

"Wait until he stops seizing." The dark-haired woman knelt beside her. "You could hurt him." She looked at her watch.

The jerking subsided, and in a moment, Max lay trembling, sweating, unconscious.

"Daddy?" Yulia knelt beside Grace, who put her arm around her daughter, holding her even as Max started to rouse.

"I called 911," Ronnie said, also nearby.

Max's eyes opened. Grace held his handsome face between her mittens. "Max. You're okay. You had a seizure. But you're okay. Just breathe."

His beautiful brown eyes searched hers, as if confused. She pressed her forehead to his. "You're okay, Max. You're okay."

Beside her, Yulia softly cried. A siren whined in the distance.

"Total time for the seizure was two minutes, forty-seven seconds," said the woman next to her. "Can I take his pulse?"

Grace backed away and looked at her.

"Dr. Aria Silver," she said. "We're just in town for the holidays."

Oh. Grace had nothing as Dr. Silver pressed her fingers to his neck. The ambulance showed up and Peter went from player to his role as fire chief, helping Ronnie and one of their town's flight nurses, Jack Stewart, load Max onto a gurney. The other players stood around, their expressions grim.

"How'd it happen?" she asked as Kyle closed the door. She hadn't been watching.

And that's when she noticed that Ivy hadn't followed her to the ice. No, she sat with her son, Tiger, who had crumpled near the goal, drawn up his knees, his arms over his head, sobbing.

"Tiger accidentally slammed into him. Lost control or something, and suddenly Max went down," Kyle said quietly.

Darek skated over to his son.

"It's not his fault," Grace said, but she didn't have time to comfort him. She looked at Yulia. "Let's go."

She ran out to the car, but as they reached the Denali, Yulia stopped her, grabbing her wrist. "Mom!"

Grace turned to her, spotted the tears in her eyes.

"Is he going to die?"

Oh. Grace pulled her against herself, her arms tight around her shoulders. "No, honey." But yes. Too soon, yes. She closed her eyes, hearing the prognosis.

Once you start showing symptoms, you'll have about seven years until the end.

Not enough time. But she swallowed, shook the words away. Forced her voice steady. "Daddy's going to be okay." She held her daughter away from her and kissed her forehead. Gave her a closed-mouth smile.

But as they got in the car, fear settled in her soul and spoke.

There would never again be a perfect Christmas.

How could Jace just sit there, almost smiling as if he might be listening to a scouting briefing of the opposite team, that glint of challenge in his devastating blue eyes? Did he not *hear* their ob-gyn?

Maybe it was Eden's fault. She too wore a strange expression, she knew it, but she was still sorting it all out. Give her a minute to just...breathe.

Outside the window, the sky hovered low and gray over the Minneapolis skyline and the forecast called for a few flurries. Hopefully it would head north and blanket Deep Haven with a layer of snow.

Through the other window, toward the waiting room, seven-year-old Emmie, her blonde hair pulled back into a wispy ponytail, presided over the castle that Sullivan and Mace were building. The boys looked so much alike—with Jace's blue eyes, her blonde hair, their crazy, lopsided grins—that sometimes, when they slept, she couldn't tell them apart. But in the daylight, oh, she knew. Sully had Jace's grit, his inability to do anything halfway. Drove his twin brother, Mace, crazy as Sully dragged the quieter, more serious version of Jace and Eden into trouble.

Poor Mace had already broken his arm, gotten stitches twice, and added near concussion to his list of injuries. Thankfully, he was also as tough as his father, who once upon a time played the position of enforcer for the Minnesota Blue Ox hockey team.

Jace was also kind and gentle and sweet and steadfast and always, always had the right words to say.

Until right now, apparently, when he went silent at the doctor's words.

"Eden?"

Oh, it was her turn. This was easy. "The answer is no. Of course no. Never, ever."

Jace slipped his hands to hers and squeezed them. Nodded at

the woman who had delivered the twins in an emergency C-section.

She was also the one who said that, because of the damage, Eden might never get pregnant again.

"It'll be high-risk, too, you know," Dr. Olivia Pike said. "So, you'll spend the last two months on bed rest, most likely. That's at the height of the Stanley Cup run, Jace."

"I'll figure something out," Jace said in his signature stalwart tone, along with a smile.

She too should smile, but inside, honestly, she shook.

It's not too late.

No. Never, ever.

But Dr. Olivia's other words couldn't be as easily repelled.

The tests indicate that your child will be born with Down syndrome.

Deep breath. She'd met plenty of amazing children with Down syndrome.

"And you did hear me about the heart problems? It is unlikely your child will survive outside the womb."

"I understand." Through the window, she spotted Sully, his blond hair tousled, wearing a Thor T-shirt, standing on the back of the sofa, arms out. Emmie was blocking him, tough older sister in a dress and leggings, hands on her hips, yelling, her voice muffled through the glass.

Mace stood over the city of blocks they'd created, his arms out too.

"What on earth—I'll be right back," Jace said and left the room.

"Are you sure this is what you want?" Dr. Pike said to Eden as Jace played referee.

"Yes, of course. This baby is a gift. It's just..." She glanced at the chaos outside. "The twins are a handful. And Jace travels so much with the team..." Her eyes burned. "I'm just not sure how I'm going to handle all this."

Stupid tears. Her mother had six children—six. And sure, none of them were special needs, but hello—*six*.

"This *is* a miracle baby," Dr. Pike said. "But it will also be a miracle if he lives outside the womb, so I just wanted you to be aware of your options."

"Not an option for us, but..."

"Then I have a support group you might want to consider attending." Dr. Pike turned and opened a drawer in her credenza. Pulled out a brochure. Set it on the desk.

A little white and red paper bomb. Eden stared at it.

Jace opened the door and poked his head in. "We probably need to go, Eden. Sully was about to take out the city with his fiery dragon breath, and Mace was ready to defend it until the end. I think I just saved this office from Armageddon."

Jace was so painfully handsome standing there in his jeans, and suit coat, a big man with an even bigger heart, the kind of guy who wasn't afraid to dive into a battle to protect his team—which now included his family. Sully was now safely imprisoned on his back. In the next room, Mace and Emmie were putting away the blocks.

Go. Get on with life. Smile.

"Thank you, Dr. Pike." Eden shoved the brochure into her purse.

"You okay, hon?" Jace said when they reached the hallway.

She looked up at him. She'd successfully blinked the burn of threatening tears away. Found herself. She could do this. "Of course. We're having a baby." She put her hand over her barely showing belly.

He put his arm around her and kissed her forehead.

Jace. Everything inside her wanted to turn and just hold onto him, but as soon as Jace put him down, Sully and Mace broke out into an impromptu 40 and raced down the hall.

"Sully—!" Jace shouted.

"Mace—!" Eden echoed.

Inside her purse, her phone rang. She let Jace run after the boys and pulled it out. "Hey, Mom. What's up?"

"Eden. I don't know if Grace has texted you—she's been pretty busy with all the tests and taking care of Max but—"

"What's wrong with Max?" Eden stilled, put a hand on her chest.

"He fell today. On the ice—"

"He was *skating?*"

"He's been doing really well, honey. Steady, no shaking, his mind clear—"

"But skating, Mom. On ice! Did he hit his head?"

"Yes, no...he had a seizure."

Emmie had pulled out an Elsa doll from her Frozen backpack and was now walking her down the hallway while Jace rounded up the boys. Eden signaled to Jace, then stepped into the women's bathroom.

"Oh no. How bad was it?"

"Thankfully, there was a doctor in the stands. And the CRT got him to the hospital pretty quickly. But he bit his tongue badly, and of course, Grace thinks his Huntington's has finally broken through all their current treatments. She's devastated."

No doubt. Eden stared at herself in the mirror—oh, she needed a haircut. And a tan. And how could she be thinking about herself when her sister's world was imploding? Sheesh.

She turned away and walked into a stall. Closed the door.

"What's his prognosis?"

"She doesn't know yet. But I was thinking that maybe..."

"Yes." Her throat tightened.

A pause. "Yes?"

"We were considering coming up early anyway—we'll be there tomorrow."

"Oh honey, I know she'll be so glad to see you. She needs us now."

"Of course, Mom."

They all knew this was coming—Max had informed Grace of his illness long before they got married. And they'd had seven amazing years together. Not that they didn't deserve more but...

No, they definitely deserved more.

Her mother's voice softened. "You okay, Eden?"

Not even a little. But she wasn't about to spill out her problems when her sister's world was shattering.

"I'm great. Everything's fantastic."

Eden ran her hand over her belly, small that it was. Small, tiny, precious. A miracle.

"Good. At least I have one daughter I don't have to worry about." Her mother gave a laugh, as if she didn't worry about them all, every day.

Eden had learned that truth when Emmie was born.

Still, "No, you don't have to worry, Mom. Everything is under control here. I'll see you tomorrow."

Then she hung up the phone, hit her knees in front of the porcelain throne, and promptly, decidedly...threw up.

Of course, Casper was late again.

Not that there was a magic time to appear in a hospital waiting area, but the rest of the family had assembled long ago, according to Raina's texts—all 5 of them—and by the time Casper had walked into the area, they'd already heard the doctor's report.

Grace was back in Max's room.

Ingrid, his mother, was on the phone with Eden.

John, his father, was talking with Darek about some broken lights on the massive Evergreen Resort Christmas tree.

Darek nodded at Casper as he came in. Of course, Darek still wore his hockey duds—yes, Casper was well aware of the fact he'd missed the game again this week.

But he had a house to finish.

In the next seven days.

Because he'd made promises to his wife, Raina, who now rose, baby Rhett on her hip. Seven-year-old sister, Layla, kneeled on the floor, coloring in a book propped on the chair. Layla looked up. "Daddy!"

He opened his arms for her and caught her up just as Raina walked over, gave him a look.

"Sorry."

"I called three times. I texted five. Where have you been?"

"The house. I finished installing the shower fixture. Sorry—I left my phone downstairs."

He spotted the disbelief in her eyes, so, "The fixture didn't fit right, so I had to go to the hardware store and get more putty, and then rig a different fitting, and—"

"Max fell."

Right. Focus on the important stuff. Like, their worst nightmares had finally found them. He set down Layla, who ran back to her book, and took Rhett from Raina. His wife wore her dark hair back in a long ponytail, a flannel shirt and jeans and was as beautiful today as the day he spotted her on a dirt road delivering pizzas.

She reached for him, and he pulled her in as she hung on. "It'll be okay."

"I don't think so," she said as she let him go. "The meds he was on aren't working, and the doctor came out and said that when he woke, he didn't know where he was."

"Is that a symptom of Huntington's?"

"It can be." His father walked over with Darek. "Cognitive issues are a sign of progression. The doc thinks that when he fell, it triggered the seizure which triggered the cognitive problems. It's all a part of the horrible stew of the disease."

"He was doing so well," Casper said. "I thought the new drugs were helping."

They all went quiet then because Grace came down the hall into the waiting area. She held Yulia's hand. "He's sleeping. But he did recognize us, and he seems to be coming back to himself."

She walked into her mother's embrace, who'd hung up the phone.

Casper couldn't watch her cry. Even Darek turned away.

"Ivy went back to the house with Joy. Tiger is packing up the gear—I'd better get back and help him," Darek said.

Right.

"How's the house coming along?"

The money pit? Casper wanted to say. He'd only owned the Wilder home for seven years and hadn't yet moved in. Yes, it took a year to unsnarl the probate and get the title free and clear. And then there were the permits. For a while there, Casper sweated it out as the city debated declaring it a historical site. But no, they gave him the free and clear to renovate the old Victorian that was once owned by the founder of Deep Haven.

It was then that he'd discovered the entire foundation had cracked. If he hadn't inherited it, then he might have walked away right then, but the wind scurried through the tiny bungalow they'd purchased in town and with Raina's dreams of a large family, this felt like the right place. So, he spent one entire summer trapped in the creepy dirt basement, jacking up the house and fortifying said foundation. And then, of course, the asbestos abatement took another year, what with the cold weather creeping in and the systematic demolition of the green wallpapered walls and ceilings.

It would help if Raina didn't want to keep every inch of beautiful oak molding, along with the hickory built-ins and kitchen cupboards, so he'd pried each piece of wood off like it might be a relic left by some ancient explorer. He'd taken up the red carpet that ran through the house, revealing the gorgeous oak flooring, and removed the Tiffany lighting in the kitchen.

Stored it all in the barn behind the house.

Of course, it all had to be done in the less-than-freezing season between April and October. During the winters, he refinished the cabinetry and built-ins he'd taken down while he waited for the new furnace and ductwork to be installed.

Then came the remodel. Done by yours truly, one exhausting room at a time—from reframing when they opened the kitchen to the living room, to rewiring, to the insulation, drywall, taping, mudding, sanding, painting, and then came the three bathrooms...

A part of him hated this house. To its bones. Sure, it would be gorgeous—was nearly ready to move in—but it had cost him hours playing with Layla and helping Raina with baby Rhett and frankly, what good was all the money he'd earned from finding Thorsen Wilder's treasure if he couldn't spend it?

But there was a shortage of contractors in Deep Haven, and Raina lived with the grand hope of college for her two children and...

And Casper liked things done right. Which meant he now owned a garage full of tools and equipment—a win, really—and knew every nook and wire and pipe in the house.

Including today's shower fixture. So, in answer to Darek's question—

"It's coming along. I promised Raina we'd be in by Christmas eve, so..."

Darek raised an eyebrow. "Seven days?"

"I finished the master bath plumbing today. Even tested it— everything works. Now, I just need to install the mirrors, the toilet, finish painting the trim, and clean the fireplace and...I intend to keep that promise."

"I never thought you'd outwork me, bro. But that house transformation is amazing."

"Thanks," Casper said. He cast a look at Raina who stood talking with Grace and his mother, now. "But being gone so much hasn't exactly been great for things between me and Raina. Ever since..." And he stopped himself.

They didn't know. None of the family. Mostly because they'd been handling a different emergency a year ago, and by the time Raina's own personal tragedy was over, she couldn't face it.

So, he'd kept quiet and gone back to work.

"Since...?" Darek said.

"Nothing. Just. It's been a busy year. Maybe moving into the house will help."

Darek clamped him on the shoulder. "Probably. Let me know if you need any help."

Like Darek had time to help him paint trim. He had enough on his plate running the Evergreen Resort, which, under his care, was rebuilt after the massive forest fire ten years ago to running at full capacity this week.

Sometimes, when Casper looked at his oldest brother, he thought he caught a glimpse of the man his father had been. Sure. Solid. Always with the right words, able to solve the family's problems. They even looked alike, with their dark hair, although his father's was graying, but same build.

Darek, the spitting, capable image of his father. He probably wouldn't be drowning in house repairs.

"Thanks," Casper said, but any request for help stuck in his throat.

Darek left and he should go too. There was nothing he could do here, really. He walked over to Raina, pulled her away. "Are you staying?"

"For a while. Rhett and I will stay with Grace. Can you take Layla?"

Aw, he'd really wanted to get started on painting the trim, but— "Sure." He pulled his dark, curly-haired seven-year-old into his embrace. He gave her a kiss on the nose. "Wanna help Daddy paint trim?"

"Yeah!" She high fived him.

He walked over to Grace and pulled her tight, one armed. "Love you, sis. Call if you need anything."

She too pressed her hand to his cheek. "Stop by and see him tomorrow, okay?"

"Yep."

He kissed Raina on the way out and Layla climbed into the second row of his pickup.

He wouldn't actually start painting, but he'd get all the supplies and drop them off at the house so he could start early tomorrow morning.

The bell jangled above the door of the hardware store as he walked in. He raised a hand to Henry Decker, probably home from college for break, working behind the counter, then headed to the back for supplies. Gave Layla a brush to hold, which she used to paint everything she could reach while he had his paint mixed.

By the time they reached the house, the sun hung on the backside of the day, casting a rosy glow upon the old mansard-roofed farmhouse on the hill. Without snow, the house was forlorn and barren amidst a yard of yellow grass, the trees skeletal in the forest around it. Someday he'd paint the barn white, as well as give the house a fresh coat.

He got out and grabbed his paint supplies.

Layla ran up the steps and into the unlocked house.

Casper stood for a moment, caught in the splendor of the twilight against the house. Once upon a time, Aggie and Thorsen Wilder had raised a family here.

A wide porch ran the perimeter of the house. Casper pictured rocking chairs on it in the summertime. And in the winter, boughs of fir wrapped around its banister.

The crowning touch would be the massive home-cut Christmas tree he'd bring in from the forest around the house and set up in the room with the turret, decorated, lit and glowing out the front window.

Yes, this house would be the perfect Christmas present for his amazing, long-suffering, beautiful wife and children. Worth it. Every exhausting minute…

"Daddy!"

Layla met him at the door as he came up the porch stairs. She still wore her mittens, but at a glance he noticed they were soaking wet, as were her shoes and pants. What—?

"Layla, why are you wet?"

But even before he opened the door, he heard it—the very wrong sound of water running—no *falling*, as if the spring thaw had let loose the snow from the nearby hills to flood the creeks and riverbeds of the north.

"Oh—!" Casper pushed inside.

A waterfall spilled from a crack in the ceiling right below the master bathroom. Right onto his beautiful, and now buckling, refinished oak floors. Drywall hung from the ceiling, ready to drop, and the water had already filled the entire lower level.

And that's when his daughter finally answered him, standing behind him in the freezing lake, her cute little pink Uggs soaking wet. "It's raining, Daddy. It's raining in the house."

2

She didn't mean to walk into their conversation. In fact, if she could have, Amelia would have stopped herself, hit reverse and backed down the hallway.

But she promised Grace coffee and she'd been head down, eyes on the donuts she balanced on each cup, and hadn't even realized that the voices she heard belonged to her parents until...

Until she spotted them tucked away in an alcove in the hallway.

They clammed up immediately as Amelia walked by and she'd never seen such a stricken look on her mother's face. Her father had a hand on her mother's arm, as if trying to convince her of something, and the entire thing looked...well, the pair was definitely keeping a secret.

Which was why Amelia backtracked to the words she'd overheard.

"We have to tell them. They deserve to know," her mother had said.

"Not yet. There's so much going on—"

"What are you going to do, wait until after you're gone? It's not fair—"

And that's when, of course, Amelia walked by. Spotted the guilt, or maybe fear? On her mother's face as she stopped talking. Everything inside Amelia clenched then, even as she kept going to Max's room.

What are you going to do, wait until after you're gone?

Yeah, those worse clung to her like a burr as she handed Grace the coffee. Max was still asleep—they'd given him a sedative for his seizure, and probably other medicine too. He looked so capable despite being dressed in a hospital gown, an IV running in his arm. Big, strong, handsome with his dark hair, a scruff of whiskers on his chin. He was still every bit as hot as when he played for the Blue Ox and was the poster boy for Huntington's disease.

The whole thing stunk. Another shade of evil in the world, and sometimes it all felt too overwhelming.

Amelia handed Grace the coffee. Yulia sat in the other chair, earbuds in, watching something on her phone. For once, Grace wasn't bothering the poor girl about getting lost in her phone. Layla was reading a book in the recliner, waiting to go to her grandparents' house.

"How are you doing?"

Red streaked Grace's eyes, but she'd stopped crying. "He was doing so well. I called his doctor at Mayo—he made him an appointment in a couple weeks, but..." Grace wrapped her arms around herself. "He was taking this new drug and seemed to be doing so well... I can't believe this happened. It's sooner than his father, and his brother is already in the final stages, so..."

Amelia looked at her cup. "I'm so sorry, sis."

Grace glanced over at her. "Thanks. Have you heard from Roark recently?"

"He emailed last night. They finished digging another well in the village we've been working in, and last night, they killed a goat and celebrated."

"You live such a different life."

"What? You don't eat goat meat and crawfish for Sunday dinner?" Amelia lifted up her donut. "For the record, I still prefer this. But you get used to the food. And the lifestyle. It's quieter. Simpler. Harder, for sure, but helping people see and know God can't be compared."

"I'm glad you decided to stay after Ree's wedding, though. Mom and Dad have really been missing you. How's the wedding planning coming?"

Right. That. It might help if they set a date. But it never felt convenient—not once over the past six years—to stop their lives and get married. Especially with all the struggle in the villages of Nigeria where they currently worked.

And now this thing with Max. And maybe...

"By the way, have you noticed Mom and Dad acting weird about anything?"

Grace shook her head. "No. Just the usual hustle around Christmas preparations. Oh, they did go out of town for a week in October. Down to Mayo. I think Dad had a checkup."

"At Mayo Clinic?"

Max stirred, and Grace got up.

What are you going to do, wait until after you're gone?

Something was wrong with Dad. And he wasn't talking. But how could he? Especially now, with Max...

Amelia went cold.

We have to tell them. They deserve to know.

What if Dad was dying?

What he deserved was to have everyone he loved home with him for Christmas.

Amelia got up and left the room just as her parents came in.

She almost stopped. Almost asked. But even as her father

23

walked over to Max's bed and touched his leg, concern on his face, she got it.

Well, they weren't going to suffer alone.

She headed down the hall, all the way to the lobby and walked outside. The sky was bruising, lights out over the harbor, glistening on the dark waters. The trees rustled, and the wind carried a nip.

Please, let him be at home and not out to sea. Although, this time of year, her call would probably go to voicemail.

His phone rang twice before her brother Owen picked up.

"Sis."

"Owen! Good. You're on land. Right? You're on land?"

A pause, then, "Yep, I'm on land. What's up?"

She pictured him—her handsome former hockey star brother who'd lost the eyesight in one eye, had trekked the world, and finally settled in a fishing village in Alaska, married to a crab boat captain. He was tough and dangerous and adventurous and probably never let things like families losing their only son to a snake bite dig into his soul and turn him terrified.

"Max fell."

A beat, then, "How bad is it?"

"He had a seizure. But they think the disease is progressing more quickly. But that's just the tip of the iceberg... I think Dad is sick."

"Sick? He didn't mention it last time he called."

"I don't think he's told anyone. But he went down to Mayo in October, and I overheard Mom and Dad arguing about not wanting to wait until after he's gone to say anything, and how we deserve to know—"

And now she was crying. How she'd gotten here, she didn't know, but she stood in the darkness, hiccupping back her breaths even as she told him how she'd walked in on their conversation. And, "Please, please, would you come home for Christmas?"

He was silent a long time, or maybe she just thought it, her heartbeats thundering in her ears.

Then her phone buzzed. She pulled it away to read the caller ID.

Roark. From Nigeria. Calling *now*? But with cell phone signals so spotty— "Owen, hang on. I need to put you on hold."

She took a breath to clear her voice and swiped the call open. "Roark?"

Oh, she loved his voice. Deep and steady, with that British accent and the way it could simply reach across the miles and wrap around her heart.

"Darling. I miss you. How are you? How is the wedding planning going?"

She could hear rumbling behind him, a train maybe. He might be in town, near the bank, which always had good service.

"It's terrible, Roark. Max fell. And my parents are keeping secrets from us—"

Silence. "Roark?"

"Yes, sorry. There was a pocket, and you cut out. Did you say you wanted it in the fall?"

What? "Roark, did you not hear me? No! How can you think about getting married right now?"

More silence, then, "I understand, sweetheart. You're upset about Kebe."

"I'm upset because a twelve-year-old boy, the only son of my best friend, was murdered, and we could do nothing—*nothing* to stop it. And my brother Max is dying. And my Dad... I'm upset because terrible things happen to people we love. And..." And the pain was too big, too long, too high.

"Ames..." But the phone turned spotty again, "Wait...time for..." And the call dropped.

Perfect. But he'd get it. They'd waited six years...they could wait until life was sorted out. Easier.

Safer.

She tried to return to Owen's call, but it too had dropped.

He picked back up on the first ring. "Hey. Sorry. I'm in the middle of something here, so I couldn't wait. I'm not sure I'm going to be able to make it, Ames. I have a small kerfuffle, but I'll do my best."

"Please try, O. Not to be dramatic, but it might be the last Christmas we all spend together."

He hung up, and she stood in the cold as the wind rattled her ears, watching the stars blink against the frigid canopy of night.

One star unlatched, fell to the earth, and winked out. Leaving behind it a terrible, endless black hole.

Owen shoved his chin into the neck of his own coat, feeling the chill on his cheeks, but really, throughout his entire body.

"You're calling this a small kerfuffle?"

The question came from Carpie, who stood on the dock in his oversized parka, the hood up, the frigid wind off the steel gray waters of Iliuliuk Harbor in western Alaska.

Overhead, the sun struggled against the dour cloud cover and the taste of an oncoming blizzard hung in the air, turning everything tinny and sharp.

They'd barely escaped the waters of the Bering Strait, again, and even he was rattled.

"That was my sister. Some family stuff. It can wait."

Maybe. Sorta. Amelia definitely sounded freaked out about Dad being sick. But during their phone call over Thanksgiving, he hadn't said a word about being ill—just mentioned the cool boat show he'd attended in Miami, and they'd talked boats and ships and Owen and his wife Scotty's upcoming crabbing trip to the Bering Sea.

Maybe it had been a hint to come home, but Owen simply

attributed it to the reasonable we-won't-talk-about-it worry his parents struggled with every time he and Scotty set out for their yearly four-month crab-fishing scramble.

A well-founded worry, given the way their boat, a 109-foot fishing vessel called the F/V *Wilhelmina 2*, listed to starboard as she was towed into port.

"I can see the patch," Carpie said, referring to the flimsy weld Owen had tried to make over the hull, where water was leaking into the void.

"Risked my stupid life in the high seas, hanging over the side of the boat, but it had worked...for about two hours."

Enough for them to limp closer to shore, for them to hang on until the Coast Guard could evacuate everyone, except, of course, him and Scotty.

Apparently, she clung to the idea that the captain needed to go down with the ship. Thankfully, it hadn't come to that, but the hours they'd waited for the Coast Guard's return had nearly been their end as he'd finally coaxed her into the life raft, turned on the homing beacon, and quietly and horrifyingly relived their first date.

But, like before, they'd lived, and the ship hadn't sunk to the bottom of the Arctic Ocean. And yes, they'd lost their cargo, three weeks of crabbing—that hurt—but again, they'd lived.

It occurred to him that maybe their luck was running thin. Still, score another one for the home team.

Although, it didn't feel like a victory, really, watching as the *Wilhelmina 2* sagged up to the dock, where she'd be unloaded and then brought into dry dock for repairs.

And if it were up to him, sold.

"How's Scotty? This has to be a blow after Red's death."

"Not great. After we were released from the hospital, she went home and got into bed. She's been there for the last two days. And yes, it's been cold, but I think the grief has just caught up to her. Hard to lose her father, and then her father's fishing boat, all in six months."

"He was a scrapper, Old Red was, and his daughter is the same. A hard life for a family, though," Carpie said. He was a bear of a man, grizzled, solid and serving as the Willie's mechanical engineer for twenty years, only giving it up for shore legs and his own machine shop a year ago when his wife got sick. Priorities. His words.

"It's all she knows, really. She grew up on his knee, at the helm."

The sea tug had settled the Willie at dock. The boat they'd hired to tow her in had affixed pumps to outflow the water, along with floats, but she looked like a hospital patient stuffed with wires and bandages, worn and tired, her massive hull bruised and bleeding rust with the force of the sea.

A few crab pots hadn't fallen into the sea. They'd be offloaded with the rest of the gear, then the ship would be dragged into Carpie's shop. He had a heart for sad cases just like this.

Hopefully he could coax her back to life.

"I wasn't talking about Scotty and her father. I was meanin' you, Owen. And Scotty. Angel and I need some god-grandchildren." Carpie waggled one bushy white eyebrow.

"Oh. Yeah—Scotty doesn't want kids."

"Aw, c'mon—"

"No, really. You know how she was raised. She says this life is too salty for kids—and despite what I say, she doesn't think she'll make a good mother—"

"That's not true."

"I know. But...we decided. In fact, I'm going under the knife once we get back from crabbing. Make it permanent. No oops while we're out at sea, not that anything exciting happens on a fishing boat."

Carpie laughed, but then shook his head. "Owen. That's a pretty permanent decision. Maybe—"

"I barely got her to marry me. She's not a happily ever after girl. And maybe she's right. The last thing Scotty needs is to worry about being pregnant while she's trying to keep the boat steady under thirty-foot swells, me on the deck pulling in pots."

Carpie made a face but the insurance adjuster, a man named Homer, walked over, dressed in a furry shapka, the ties blowing in the wind, and a thick canvas jacket. "I dunno, Owen. Sure you don't want to total this out? Those repairs on this old girl might be more than she's worth."

Owen clamped a gloved hand on his shoulder. "We need to fix her, get her back in the water. Preferably before the New Year. We have at least a month of fishing left, and with the last catch back in the sea—"

"It'll take at least two weeks to get her seaworthy, and that's working every day. With the holidays…even crabbers take a week off," Carpie said. "Maybe you should be taking that trip home."

Maybe. He hadn't been home since baby Layla had been born. And sure, he'd signed away his parental rights, but now that he wouldn't be having any more children, something inside him tugged at the desire to see her. Sure, Casper was her father —and a good one. But Owen held a soft place for her, thanks to Casper's pictures, texts, and updates.

Still, his life was here, with Scotty, and he didn't want her to think he might be pining for anything different.

"Get her into dry dock, Carpie, and see what you can do. Maybe we can salvage this season, yet."

"Or maybe God has a better plan for you." He winked.

Carpie. Just when Owen thought God wasn't listening, Carpie brought him back to the basics.

He wasn't in this alone, and maybe he should remind Scotty of this.

It was sinking in, but maybe it should always feel like a miracle...they'd lived.

"Before you go, Angie packaged up some stew. It's on the front seat."

Carpie walked him out to his truck, their feet crunching through the freshly packed snow. Owen's own truck hummed, still running. He was afraid to turn off the seldom run engine in this weather. Not unless it was plugged in.

Retrieving the stew in a massive Dutch oven, duct-taped closed, Carpie gave it to Owen, who set it on his floorboard.

"Merry Christmas, son. Go home. I'll take care of the *Wilhelmina*. You take care of our girl Scotty."

It felt like a pep talk, the kind he used to get before taking the ice for the Blue Ox, back when he was young and confident and thick with dreams.

He still had dreams. But mostly he had Scotty. And that was enough.

The little house on the hill, once occupied by Red, had gotten a face-lift since Owen and Scotty had moved in two years ago, after putting Red in a nearby nursing home. His stroke had rendered him unable to live by himself, and Scotty had to run the crab boat to pay for his care.

Which left Owen digging into his rusty, resort-taught repair skills. He'd opened up the kitchen of the tiny bungalow, replaced the flooring with wood, created an island, and repaired the old fireplace that, when stocked, kept the entire place humming with heat. He'd also updated the master bedroom and added a bath, which cut into the other bedroom, but since they only needed one...

He'd even repainted, then added a porch. The house was bright and cheery, the light on over the front walk as he parked the truck in the decluttered detached garage, plugged it in, and lugged the Dutch oven into the house.

He paused at the sound of Christmas music playing on a pair of Bluetooth speakers in the kitchen.

Huh.

"Scotty?"

He set the food on the stove, turned it to warm. Their front living room overlooked the massive harbor, the sun already surrendering into the last of the afternoon, just a few lights twinkling below, and in a way, it reminded him of the view of Deep Haven, at the top of Pincushion Mountain. All he missed were the red and green twinkle lights of Main Street.

Okay, so maybe Amelia's call had dredged up a stir of nostalgia. But his dad was fine, and Max was...well, there wasn't anything he could do about Max.

Except, pray, really. He had a life here.

And a *wife* here, who was deep in the throes of a weird, dark funk.

"Scotty?"

He walked into the bedroom. Stopped.

Open on the bed was a suitcase, a couple sweaters, jeans, a pair of dress boots from her Anchorage days, and a bag of toiletries piled inside.

He stared at it, not sure... "Honey?"

"In here."

He followed her voice to the bathroom. She pulled back the curtain on the tub and stuck her head out. "Hey, champ."

"Hey." She was in the *bath*? Her dark hair was wet, and steam rose from the top of the curtain. "Whatchya doin'?"

She gave him a look. "Well I'm not trying to keep warm in the middle of the ocean."

"No, you're not. What did you do—set the water on boil?"

She smiled, and at once the darkness cleared. He hadn't seen her smile in so long he'd sorta forgotten how she could part the clouds, let the sunshine in.

"Almost. And I added bubbles."

"Who are you and what have you done with my salty, sea-brined wife?"

"She's leaving you."

What—?

She laughed again. "Unless you want to join her."

"Always. But where are we going?" he said and pulled off his sweater.

Her eyes widened. "Um. Well, I thought maybe we'd go to Deep Haven. See your family for Christmas."

Huh. But he wasn't going to ask any questions, except the important one. He unsnapped the button on his pants. "Any room in there for me?"

Someone had gone overboard with the Christmas lights while he was away. Sure, Darek had put up the red, green, and blue twinkle lights along his roof line, but now, as he pulled into the driveway of his small house in town, he noticed the front lamp post was wrapped, along with the mailbox, and somehow Ivy had erected a massive star on their roof. But what really caught his eye was the giant blow-up Santa, a sleigh, and eight not-so-tiny reindeer in his front yard.

Sheesh, a guy was late for dinner and his front yard blew up in some kind of epic light show. Maybe it was Ivy's holiday cheer fix for their lack of snow.

He got out, not wanting to think about the electric bill, and headed inside through the side door. The kids' jackets hung on hooks, the shoes neatly lined up. He peeled off his own attire, smelling something delicious from the kitchen, and his stomach roared to life.

Sinatra sang "Let it Snow!" from the house speaker, and he noticed the table set as he walked into the kitchen.

They'd waited.

Ivy was at the sink, dressed in jeans and a Christmas sweater, and wearing an apron. Apparently, he'd entered a Lifetime movie.

"Sorry I'm late."

"It's okay. I know the resort comes first." She turned, wiped her hands, and lifted her pretty face for a kiss. The bells on her silly Christmas sweater jangled, and she wore her red hair down. She looked so ridiculously gorgeous he felt like a beast out of the wilderness in his flannel and dirty jeans.

And a little of that beast seemed to awaken as he kissed her.

Oh, he was a blessed man. He knew it every day, down to his soul. "The resort doesn't come first, Ives. Just—"

"Listen. I know the rules of hospitality." She pressed her hands on his chest. "Did you get the lights on the tree fixed?"

Her comment sat in his bones, but he shook it away. "It has enough lights to see from space."

"At least the resort has guests. What we really need is some Christmas snow," Ivy said. "Tiger! Joy!" she hollered down the hallway. "We waited."

"I see that. Sorry I took so long. I stayed at the hospital until we got a prognosis."

"Which is?"

"Not great. I hate that they're going through this."

Tiger came into the room, his eyes still red. Darek put his arm around his shoulder. "It's not your fault, okay? Max has a disease—we all know this. And he was on borrowed time. It just triggered—"

"When I slammed into him," Tiger said, not looking at his dad.

"Maybe. Or maybe it was already happening, and *he* was the one out of control. Ever think of that?"

Tiger shook his head. "He's a pro skater, Dad."

"And a pro knows that this happens on the ice. Let it go."

Tiger drew in a breath, swallowed. Nodded.

But Darek didn't buy it. The kid was like him—regrets clung to him.

Ivy came over, carrying a casserole dish. "I made your mother's chicken festival." She set the dish on the table, beside rice and broccoli and fresh rolls and—

And then he got it. "You got the appointment."

She turned, grinned.

"Judge Ivy!" He picked her up, twirled her around. "Seriously?"

"It's just until the election, but—"

"That's fantastic. I'm so proud of you." He set her down, caught her face in his hands, kissed her again.

"Ew," said Joy as she came to the table. "Yuck."

Ivy laughed, and Darek let her go, then turned to his daughter. Strawberry blonde braids, a fuzzy white sweater with a Christmas tree on it, leggings and wool socks. Seven years old and she owned his heart. "Mommy said that you got a library card this week."

"She brought home a stack of books that will probably keep her in her room for the rest of Christmas vacation," said Ivy as she sat down.

"I've already read two of them!" Joy said.

"Smart, just like your mom." Darek winked.

Tiger said nothing next to her. He too was as smart as his mother, but a different mother, and sometimes Darek forgot that comments like that dug a hole in Tiger. Only recently he'd expressed sadness in not knowing her.

Regrets.

But then Darek would have never had Joy, or Ivy, and…oh, it was too hard to choose really. He was just thankful that in the end, God looked down on him and picked up the pieces.

Darek prayed for them, then dug into the chicken.

"When do you start the appointment?"

"Maybe the end of January." Ivy passed him the rice. "I talked with Nathan today and he said we could probably put the house up for sale by the first of the year. With the housing market—"

"What?" Oh, he didn't mean his tone the way it came out, but... He took a breath. "Did you say put the house up for *sale?*"

She had frozen, her eyes wide. "Um. Well, I thought with us moving..." She met his gaze. "Or maybe we're not moving."

Darek cast a glance at Tiger. Joy wouldn't be upset by a move, but Tiger—he had a life here. Coached peewee hockey and played for his own team, as well as the family, and... "What about the resort?"

Oh, he wished he hadn't started with that because Ivy drew in a breath. "I get it. I really do. But I thought...it's such a long drive."

"Listen. You and our family are more important than the resort, and I would follow you anywhere, Ives. But we have a life here, and so do our kids. And it's only a year. What if you commute for a month, and if it doesn't work, then...we move."

He actually said the last words without his voice dipping. Move. The word felt like a bullet through his chest.

He'd already given up the cabin to rent out that he'd built for their personal home at the resort in favor of a house in town, closer to Ivy's job and the kids' school. But leave Deep Haven... leave the *resort?*

She drew in a breath. "It's a three-hour drive, one way. That's six hours on the road every day, Darek."

Right.

"And what if I win the election?"

He blinked at her. Win. The. *Election?* "You're going to run?"

She had put down her fork now, and he wondered if maybe he should ask the children to leave. Or maybe they should leave and step outside.

Because he knew his attorney wife and she was probably right. And even if she wasn't, she was about to remind him that she had thought through *everything.*

Ah, and now he got it—the Christmas decorations were the last great Christiansen family display.

She settled her voice, and he heard the lawyer in it. "Of course I'm going to run. I've wanted this judgeship for...well, it's a dream, really. Why would I give that up after a year—"

"Because our life is here?" And again, he winced. He was just tired, and seeing Grace's life disintegrating had put him on the sharp edge of stress.

Apparently, it was running in the family.

"Our life could be there."

"I run the family resort. The one that has been around for nearly *one hundred years*."

"I know, but...your dad is there, and maybe Casper could help out..." Her mouth pinched and she looked away.

And shoot, deployed the clincher—tears.

Tears! Not fair, counsel.

But Ivy wasn't a manipulator—not ever. So, "I didn't realize this meant that much to you."

"I guess I didn't either," she said quietly. "Until I got the call today." She wiped her eyes with her napkin.

And that was just it. He stood up and reached for her hand. Looked at the kids. "Stay here."

Then he pulled his wife down the hall to their bedroom and closed the door. She leaned against it, looking up at him. Her eyes were still thickened with tears.

He touched her chin. "Babe. I didn't realize..." Then he touched his forehead to hers. "If this is what you really want, then...okay. We'll figure it out. Maybe I come down on weekends and help, or...yes, Casper can help. Or Dad can hire someone..." He offered a smile, all those ideas sitting like a fist in his chest.

But he was a blessed man.

She put her hands on his chest. "Really?" So much softness, so much gratefulness in her voice.

36

"Really." He met her eyes, smiled, and shoot, couldn't stop himself from kissing her.

Wow he loved this woman. And when she sighed and wrapped her arms around his neck, her little bells jangling, it was all he could do not to let supper go cold.

"Best thing I ever did was buy you, Darek Christiansen," she said when he lifted his head.

"You did not buy me."

"Yeah, I did." She winked. "Most eligible bachelor in Deep Haven." Then she wiggled out of his embrace and headed back to the kitchen.

Maybe she did. Because she owned every inch of him.

Now, he just had to tell his father that he was leaving the Christiansen resort.

Yeah, this would be a fun Christmas.

3

Her mouth was cotton, every bone in her body ached, the man she loved lay in a hospital bed, and over the hallway loudspeakers, Andy Williams was telling her it was the most wonderful time of the year.

Not even a little. But for Max, and Yulia, she'd fake it.

In fact, last night after the family had left and Max had fallen asleep and Yulia left with her grandma, Grace had headed to their quiet home on the hill. She whipped up a dozen of Max's favorite brown sugar muffins, bagged them, grabbed her pillow, and headed back to his hospital room.

They'd kept him overnight for observation, but really, they could have left any observation to Grace, at their home in his own bed, because she sat in the recliner until dawn slipped into the room. She'd finally given way to sleep when a nurse came in and checked his vitals, yet again, and confirmed that he was stable.

For now.

She roused as the morning breakfast cart rattled into the room. Took a breath and opened her eyes, scrubbing her hands down her face.

"Hey there, beautiful." The voice was low, soft, thick with emotion, and she looked up to see that Max had awakened.

Oh, he was handsome, even dressed in a flimsy hospital gown, two days of dark beard growth on his chin, his dark hair tousled and a little long, like he'd worn it when he played pro hockey.

Back when his face was on posters and tickets and when she sat in the family section of the stands waiting for him to skate by and send her a wink. Her entire body would turn hot, knowing that this amazing man, who defied odds and pushed through darkness, had chosen to walk through life with her.

No matter how long, or short, it might be.

He greeted the young female orderly with a smile as she pushed up the bedside stand and set the pink breakfast tray on it.

"Room service. Gotta love this place," Max said as he reached for the cover. The girl laughed, and clearly Max still had fans, if not his public charm.

Powdered eggs, apple juice, and dry toast.

"I brought Miracle Muffins," Grace said and reached for the plastic container in her bag.

"You're the miracle," he said and caught her hand as she put the box on the tray. Then he pulled her close and kissed her cheek. "Sorry," he said quietly.

Oh, her eyes burned, and she blinked fast. "Max. Sorry for what?"

He leaned back even as she opened the container. The last thing he needed was to see her cry.

"For not telling you that...that things were getting worse."

She looked at him, nonplussed. "But...you were doing so well. You went skating—"

"Denial."

The word sat like a bomb between them. She was holding a

muffin and now sat down on the chair, setting it on her lap. "Denial."

"This wasn't the first seizure. I found myself on the bathroom floor a week ago. And a few days ago I sat in front of the computer for an hour trying to remember a word. Just blanked out. Couldn't even remember what I was doing."

"Maybe it's stress," she said softly.

"Grace. I live the least stressed life of anyone I know. You take care of everything. The only stressful thing I do is sign autographs to support the Huntington research foundation."

He meant it, because his signature had started to shake with the chorea that came with his disease.

His blue eyes met hers, and his mouth twitched up. "I stopped taking the tetrabenazine."

The words were a punch, right in her sternum. "What? Max —that's the only drug that works."

"It doesn't work. It makes me depressed, and I can't sleep and I feel like I have a cold, constantly, not to mention the headaches—"

"But it keeps you alive!" She didn't mean to shout. Or turn her muffin to crumbs.

"I stopped taking it two months ago."

She looked away, her eyes blurred. Shook her head. And then, she simply couldn't stop herself. "You're a jerk."

Silence fell between them, and she closed her eyes.

She didn't mean it, of course, because Max just might be the most considerate, sweetest man she'd ever met. But—

"I didn't want to do something that would destroy us."

She looked at him, not caring now that tears ran down her cheeks. "You dying will destroy us!"

"I will die, Grace." His expression turned serious, his game face on, and it shot a ripple of fear through her. "Sooner than later. But I don't want to hate my life on the way there."

"You hate your life?"

"I did on the tetrabenazine. I'm sorry, Grace, I know I should have told you, but—"

"I saw it."

He frowned.

"I should have known. I saw you, happier, these past two months. Embracing life again." She wiped her cheek. "But if you don't take it..."

"I'll get worse, sooner." He reached out for her, and she took his hand. "But I'd rather be happy with you now, than linger and being, well, a jerk. That can't be my legacy."

Oh Max. "That will never be your legacy."

But this couldn't be the answer.

He scooted over in the bed. "There's room here."

She set her crumbled muffin on the tray and pushed it aside. Slid into the space beside his still-strong body on top of the blanket, set her head on his chest, and listened to him breathe.

He slid his arm around her, his fingers woven into hers on his chest.

She could stay here forever. And maybe he was right. They needed good memories, happy memories.

She closed her eyes, and for a moment, she was in Hawaii, where they'd met, him teaching her how to snorkel, chasing a turtle out to sea. Or eating poke bowls, or later, finding and adopting Yulia.

They already had a lifetime of happy memories.

But greedily, she wanted more. More of Max.

She had to find a way to hang onto their happy ending.

"Oh, I'm sorry to interrupt."

Grace lifted her head to see the dark-haired doctor from the ice rink standing at the door. Behind her stood a blond man dressed in a winter jacket.

"Can we come in?"

Grace got off the bed and stood up. "Max, this is—oh, shoot, I can't remember—"

"Dr. Aria Silver, and this is my husband, Jake. We were in town, on our way home from skiing, and I wanted to stop by and see how you're doing." She walked in. Petite, her dark hair down, she possessed an air of confidence as she glanced at the vitals board written on the wall.

"Better," Max said. "Did we win?"

"It really wasn't fair that we had a pro hockey player against us," said the blond. But he grinned and held out his hand. "Jake Silver. Massive fan."

Max shook it, the words eking out a smile. "Thanks."

"So, I don't mean to interfere," Dr. Silver said, "Except, it's sort of what I do...so I talked with the physicians here, and then made a call to Dr. Hayes at Mayo."

"You know Max's doctor?"

"He's a good friend of mine. He mentioned a gene therapy trial that's just starting. It seeks to silence the production of the mutant Huntington protein—so it's not a cure, but it can slow the disease way down. It's hard to get into but I could pull a few strings—"

"No."

The word from Max was a stab through the hope in the air.

Grace looked at Max, the set of his jaw and the frame of his mouth. Oh no.

"No. I'm not going to spend hope on a trial that is bound to fail."

"Max—" Grace started

"No." Max folded his arms. "I know all about the AMT-130 trial. It's supposed to repentantly change my genetic makeup and introduce new DNA that tells my body not to make the Huntington's protein."

"That's exactly—"

"Part of the trial is to drill into my skull, while I'm awake, to administer the medicine."

Oh.

He took her hand, squeezed it, then turned to Dr. Silver. "Thank you so much, doctor, for all you did and your help, but I don't want to turn into a vegetable quite yet." He smiled.

Grace looked away, her eyes burning again.

"I understand, Max." Dr. Silver said. "Well, I know they are taking a limited number of participants, so I just wanted to reach out to see if you might be a fit. This isn't an easy disease, and we respect your right to choose."

Grace didn't. Not at all.

"Have a Merry Christmas, you two."

"Hope to see you again on the ice," Jake said. "I hear there's a New Year's Day game."

He wouldn't be there. At least if she had anything to say about it.

"See you on the ice." Max fist-bumped Jake.

Had he lost his ever-lovin' mind?

Or had he reverted, again, into denial?

Jake and Aria left the room and Grace turned to Max, who'd let go of her hand and reached for a muffin.

"Seriously?"

He looked at her. "Seriously. I don't want to risk what we have—"

"For what we could have?" She was crying now, and he reached for her hand, but she yanked it away. "I just don't get you."

Then she marched out of the room.

Aria and Jake were near the lobby doors, and she caught up to them in the lobby.

"Dr. Silver!"

Aria turned. "Call me Aria, please. You have a brave man in there."

"I have stupid man in there!" Grace schooled her voice. "How long before the trial starts?"

"Right after the New Year. But the deadline for application is

in a couple days. He'd need a full checkup and a recommenda-
tion from Dr. Hayes, but I think he'd be a good candidate."

Grace nodded. "I agree. And he will too, he just doesn't
know it yet." She cut her voice low. "Save his spot and order the
tests. He will agree to the trial…I promise."

Of course, the Evergreen resort was festooned with Christmas
cheer as Eden and Jace and the kids pulled into the lot. A few
other cars were parked, guests staying at the cabins, equally
festooned. Lights hung from the massive fir in the front yard
that had survived the fire ten years ago, and twinkly lights lined
the sharp roof line and the front door of the main lodge. A
homemade wreath hung from said door, adorned with a velvety
red ribbon. Emmie, Sully, and Mace piled out of the SUV, and
ran up the steps and into the house.

She felt the same way. Somehow returning home at
Christmas always swept her out of her overwhelming life and
into a pocket of joy. This year, it was again the perfect getaway,
and for the next ten days, Eden simply *wouldn't think about* how
her life was imploding.

No, not imploding. Just took an unexpected left turn. She
would adapt. She always did.

After all, she was—at least, deep in her bones—still a Christiansen.

Still, Eden grabbed Jace's arm as he made to get out. "Not a
word."

He looked at her, frowned. "About?"

About? How about the *Thing*. The *Big News*.

Except, maybe it hadn't quite hit him like it did her. The man
was acting weird—ever since yesterday, when she'd gotten
home and declared they were leaving for Deep Haven in the

morning, five days early, he'd put on a happy face, practically humming "White Christmas" as he packed the car this morning.

"The *baby*."

Was he even paying attention to the tiny, explosive crisis in their lives?

Maybe, because he leaned over to her, met her eyes, touched her cheek, and kissed her. Quietly. Lingering.

Jace possessed a quiet power that could calm her world. Make her believe everything would be okay.

She'd be lost without him.

"It's your call, babe," he said. "But Inga and Pops will be thrilled, I'm sure."

Yes, probably. But for some reason, if she said it out loud, it became real.

And she didn't have the bandwidth at the moment for it to be real.

He got out and greeted her father, who'd come out to the porch wearing a flannel shirt, jeans, and his leather slippers. "John!"

"You're early!"

That's when Jace closed the door, so she didn't know what he'd said in response, but it wasn't hard to guess his answer.

Jace and Max had been teammates. And when one Christiansen went down, they all went down.

No, her problems were a pebble compared to the avalanche of suffering heading toward Grace, Max, and Yulia, so yes, she'd keep her mouth shut.

Besides, her mother's words hung in her mind like sap. *At least I have one daughter I don't have to worry about.*

Yep.

She got out and went around to the back right about the time Jace and her father lifted the cargo hatch. She barely caught one of the presents tumbling out.

Jace caught it with her and looked at her. "Please let me do this." He raised an eyebrow.

Fine. She wasn't an invalid, but she'd been bedridden with the twins, so maybe he was right.

She headed inside, the smells of the house nearly reeling her in as she drew close. Gingersnaps, hot cocoa, and peanut butter kiss cookies. Boots and coats mounded in the entryway, and she worked for a moment hanging them up as she listened to the kids greet their grandma.

Ingrid Christiansen—aka, Grandma Inga, or just Inga as baby Emmie had called her. It stuck. Inga and Pops had nine grandchildren and they deserved every moment of Christmas joy—the cookies, the puzzle making, the sledding and ice-skating—ice! "Mom, is the ice thick enough on the lake to skate on?"

Eden pulled off her boots and hung up her jacket. Last year, Emmie had gone out onto the ice by the dock and went in. Only Jace's close proximity had kept her from getting sucked under into the lethal darkness forever. But she'd almost lost two precious lives that day.

"Mom!"

She walked into the great room.

Her mother, the keeper of Christmas cheer, was swinging Emmie around as Elvis sang "Blue Christmas" from the speakers near the fireplace, and Sully and Mace sorted through gifts under the massive live tree that rose two stories in the great room.

A slew of stockings hung from the banister that ran upstairs to the three bedrooms, and dozens of cookies covered the big island in the kitchen.

On stools at the counter, Yulia and Layla sat frosting sugar cookies.

"Mom, did you hear—"

"Eden, honey!" Her mom turned and pulled her into a tight hug. "Welcome. I had no idea you were arriving so soon!"

Eden didn't know why, but suddenly time stopped. Maybe it was the smell of her mother—the lavender lotion on her skin—the jingle of bells on her Christmas sweater, the softness of her lips on Eden's cheek, the slight sway as she finished the hug and pulled away.

In that moment, Eden was nineteen again and coming home for Christmas, single, overwhelmed with school, and so, so glad to escape.

So glad to be home.

Her eyes filled.

"Honey. Are you okay?" Her mother pressed her hands to her cheeks, her blue eyes searching Eden's. She had this way of looking into her soul—Eden had never been able to lie to her mother like Owen or Casper or even Darek had—so she looked away.

But oh, she wanted to spill. Like Jace had said—her parents would be thrilled.

So how could she tell them that she...wasn't.

That the thought of being pregnant again was an anvil on her heart. And it wasn't just the pregnancy.

"Yes. Just tired." She found a smile, and then stepped past her mother and caught Sully as he launched himself from the top of the sofa. "Sully! I told you—no climbing!"

She set him down and noticed that Mace had found the cookies. "Mace! Not before lunch!"

Her mother caught his grimy hand en route to grabbing a cookie, wrapped him in a hug, and tickled him. "How about if Inga gets you a ham sandwich while your mom gets you settled."

Settled. As opposed to the upheaval that was her constant state of life.

She didn't know how her mother did it. If Inga and Pops had

shown up at her house unannounced, they would have found Legos and toys littering the floor, dirty dishes in the sink, piles of laundry still unfolded, and who knew what sort of growth in the fridge.

Maybe. Or maybe it would have been a good day and she would have caught up a little with the laundry, cleaning, reading aloud, and general mothering that seemed akin to managing a team of warring vikings, aka, her twins.

Mace nodded, and he and Sully climbed up on stools as Joy came off her stool to greet Emmie.

"Yulia, how are you doing?" Eden walked over to her niece who hadn't even looked up from her project. She had a nice collection of decorated bells, with red and green sugars.

Yulia lifted a shoulder.

Eden frowned and looked at her mother, who was getting out bread. "Grace called. Max had a good night. I think they are keeping him another night, although I don't know why."

Eden didn't want to ask in front of Yulia, but...

"Raina and Casper are coming for dinner, and Darek and Ivy will be here too. I'm sure Grace will have an update for us by then. Amelia went down to the hospital to check on her."

"Can I have a sandwich, too, Inga?" Sully asked.

"I *do* feed them," Eden said to her mother, who had pulled out a loaf of homemade bread.

"I know you do, honey." She looked up. "You're upstairs in the boys' room. I did some redecorating—there's a queen bed and bunks in there. And I made a bed on the floor with a mattress and your old Little Mermaid sleeping bag for Emmie."

Of course she did.

At that moment, Jace came in the door carrying their suitcases and a couple backpacks. He slid off his shoes and headed inside and Eden pointed him up the stairs.

"Hello, Inga," Jace said. He'd started calling Ingrid by her grandma name when the twins were born.

"JJ," her mother said. "In between games?"

He glanced at Eden, then back to her. "I was able to sneak away."

Thanks, Jace.

He carried the suitcases upstairs, and she followed him with the backpacks.

The room had gotten a makeover—gone was the plaid wallpaper and wooden wainscoting. Her mother had painted the room with the slanted roof all white, replaced the carpet, and added an old-fashioned metal bed and two wooden bunk beds, both with giant stuffed moose waiting for the boys.

Her mother thought of everything. Did everything.

Managed everything.

And Eden could barely remember to pack her pajamas.

In fact—

Oh shoot. Maybe she could find one of the boys' old T-shirts.

"There's something magical about the Evergreen Resort," Jace said, walking over after depositing the suitcases on the bed to wrap her in his arms. He stood at the window, looking down at the lake—where Emmie had nearly died—and kissed the top of her head. "You'll see. Everything is going to be okay."

She turned around in his arms.

"I forgot my pajamas."

He looked at her, his expression blank. Then he smiled. "In fact, I think this will be the best Christmas yet."

Casper's shout echoed through the cavernous, bare Wilder house, rattling the windows, and frankly, scaring even him.

More anger than pain, but indeed pain as he stared at his hand where the nail had gone right through the soft tissue between his thumb and forefinger.

A stupid mistake. He'd been too far extended on the ladder,

not wanting to move it and it had wobbled a second before he pulled the trigger on his gun. During that second, he'd grabbed the joist for balance, moved the gun and neatly nailed his hand to the rafter.

His eyes nearly rolled back in his head now as he reached for his hammer—thankfully tucked into his belt or he'd have to do even more damage to his hand—and pried the nail from the board.

And from his flesh.

"Oh…oh…" He huffed out breaths as he got off the ladder, then knelt on the floor, his hand over the wound lest he bleed on the floors—although the oak had warped and half the flooring in the living room would need to come up.

He blew out a breath, almost dizzy now, and grabbed a nearby rag he'd used for painting and wrapped it around his hand.

Just a flesh wound, but it hurt like the dickens, and he closed his eyes and let out another groan.

He was starting to really hate this house. Really, to his bones, a kind of hatred that had him dreaming of taking a match to it.

After he'd walked into the flood yesterday, he'd managed to turn off the water, then sop up the lake and turn on fans to dry it, although the temps outside hadn't helped. He'd returned this morning to find the makings of an ice rink in his family room.

So much fun, taking down his drywalled ceiling, and then examining the joists for damage. They seemed okay, but the wall had also warped, so he took that out too.

He'd then confirmed that there had been bad putty in the fitting, repaired the plumbing, tested it, and tore up the buckling floor under the bathroom cabinet. Which meant reinforcing the joists under it. And nailing his hand to the joist.

Which ended with him lying on the family room floor, gritting his teeth against the throbbing hand.

Of course, that's when his phone rang. He got up and

crawled over to it, swiped open the call with his knuckle. "Hey, babe."

"Casper. Are you coming for dinner? It's nearly ready—your mom made pot roast and mashed potatoes and Eden and Jace are here—"

"Yes." He glanced at his phone clock, then outside. He hadn't even noticed the darkening hour. "I'll be there in twenty minutes."

He hung up. Looked at his hand. He couldn't show up with blood. After going to the kitchen, he opened the faucet and stuck his hand under it to clean it. Nearly howled again, but managed just a few deep grunts, then he found a washcloth and wrapped it around the still running wound.

He kept a small first aid kit in his toolbox and dug around until he found some gauze and a pad. For such a small hole, the thing had really bled. But in a moment, it had started to clot, the hole closing upon itself. He put on the gauze, wrapped it around his hand, and then, because he had nothing else, secured it with duct tape.

Perfect.

Then he grabbed his keys and headed out the door.

He was hungry—his last meal being oatmeal at o-dark-early this morning. But he'd made decent progress. He could sneak back tonight and replace the plywood in the bathroom, and maybe even get drywall up on the ceiling and walls. And then he'd be back in action. Mudding, sanding, and then painting and finally installing flooring down by Christmas Eve.

He'd be able to keep his promise to Raina.

The driveway was full as he pulled up. Ivy's Escape—she must have driven Raina, because Casper had taken their only vehicle—and Jace's family SUV.

He didn't see Grace's car, but she was probably at the hospital. And the resort truck was gone, too, so maybe Darek was in town.

A little blood had seeped out under the tape, but when he wiped it off with a rag in his truck, nothing more appeared, so he was in the clear.

He got out and headed inside.

The aroma of dinner reached out and took hold of his stomach. Onions, garlic, mashed potatoes, a roast, homemade rolls, and he might even smell cookies.

This was what a home was supposed to be. Not a deluge of water in the living room.

He'd bet his father—or Darek—had never shot himself in the hand with his nail gun.

Pulling off his jacket, Casper hung it up, then shoved his hand in his pocket and entered the great room.

"Casper!" Eden was standing at the island, plating the mashed potatoes. Putting the spoon down, she walked over and hugged him. He one-armed hugged her back.

"Sis."

"You look good," she said. "Although a little dusty." She swatted off some debris from his flannel shirt.

"Working on the house," he said.

"Almost done?" Jace said, holding out his hand. Casper met it.

He was conjuring an answer when Raina walked over. "He's my handyman hero." She grabbed his lapels and kissed him. "He won't let me see it, but he promised we'd be in by Christmas."

He forced a smile. "Yep."

"Daddy!"

Layla took a leap at him, and what was he going to do, let her fall? He pulled his hand from his pocket and caught her up. Hugged her as she wrapped her arms around his neck. "I missed you!"

"I missed you, too, pumpkin."

"Is it still raining?"

Oh, pumpkin, *ixnay on the ainray*. But she was seven—he

could hardly expect her to keep a secret. He didn't look at Raina. "Nope. Daddy fixed it."

"I do wish we'd get some snow," his mother said, saving him without knowing it.

"What happened to your hand?" Raina urged Layla from his embrace. "Are you okay?"

He looked at his wound as if he'd forgotten about it. "Blister. Overkill. Wow, Mom, this smells delicious."

Ivy was setting the table, Tiger wrestling with Eden's sons, Rascal One and Rascal Two, and Yulia, Joy and Emmie were coloring on the coffee table. Layla joined them.

"Where's Darek?"

"He's getting the live nativity set up at church. He'll be here—"

The door opened behind him at her words. Casper turned, and Darek came in. "Hey."

Darek lifted a chin at him. Frowned at his taped hand but said nothing as he shed his coat.

Eden finished with the potatoes, and his mother pulled the roast from the oven. "Well, Casper, I know you've been working hard. I'm just glad you could tear yourself away."

"Every waking hour," Raina said, retrieving the rolls. "I'm beginning to feel like a widow."

Everyone laughed, but he knew she wasn't exactly kidding.

"If I know Casper, the place will be beautiful. He's been working on it for years." This from his father, who walked in from his office. He clamped a hand on Casper's shoulder. "I should have never let him get away."

Darek walked past him, glanced at him, a strange look on his face.

"Has anyone heard from Grace?" Casper picked up a dinner roll, dodging Raina as she tried to grab it away from him.

"She and Amelia are still at the hospital," his mother said.

Tiger had one of the Rascals pinned, and he was squealing

for help. The other ran over to Casper and grabbed his hand. "Help us, Unca Casp!"

He bit back a groan. "Not now, kiddo."

"Aw—"

And then Jace scooped him up and threw him over his shoulder and joined the battle by pinning all three of them.

But Darek was frowning at him. "You sure you're okay?"

"Yep. Hungry though."

His dad called them to the table and Casper found his place by Raina, and they sat down and held hands and prayed and he made it through all that without wincing. In fact, he made it through the entire dinner, plowing through the mashed potatoes and pot roast like he might be a Viking warrior back from war. Oh, he was famished.

Jace talked about the current season of the Blue Ox, and Ivy told her version of Max's accident, and his dad updated them on his last conversation with Owen, who was out at sea catching crab. Someday Casper was going to have mundane, everyday conversations around his dining room table. Yes, they wouldn't have quite the brood, but he'd fix that with the beautiful house he'd give Raina.

He started to breathe, his wound throbbing less, and by the time his mother served up the cookies, he had found his second wind.

"I gotta run," he said not long after he finished a decorated blue bell.

"Really?" Raina got up with him. "Tonight?"

He nodded, then kissed her forehead. "I'll be late." He looked at his mother. "Keep me updated on Max."

Then he headed to the door, grabbing his jacket on the way out.

He didn't expect Darek to follow him out to the truck. Or for his brother to put his hand on the door as Casper reached for it. "You're bleeding."

The outside lights emitted a glow into the yard, enough for him to see his hand. Indeed, his palm welled with blood. He'd kept his hand tucked under the table for most of dinner, so...

"I nailed it to a rafter."

Darek's eyebrows raised. "Ouch."

Casper lifted a shoulder. "I'll live."

"Need some help on the house?"

And for a second, a long second, Casper nearly nodded. Nearly surrendered to the pulse inside to ask for help.

But something about asking big brother to step in and save him... "Nope. I got this." He reached for the door handle.

Darek didn't move.

"Bro?"

Darek blew out a breath. "Okay, here's the deal." He shoved his hands into his jacket pockets. "I'm leaving the resort."

The wind shifted through the trees, a gust catching Casper's collar and spiraling down his back. "What?"

"Ivy's been appointed to a judgeship in Duluth. We're moving."

"*Moving.*" Casper knew he sounded stupid, but what—? Darek couldn't *move.*

"To Duluth."

"For how long?"

"Dunno."

"You. *Don't. Know?*"

"Could be a year. Could be longer."

Casper looked at him. "You're leaving the resort."

"Mmhmm." Darek stood in profile, looking out at the lake. The setting sun glazed it in shades of red. "You built this place. It's as much yours as it is Mom and Dad's."

Darek drew in a breath. Nodded.

"Are you sure?"

"Not even a little." He turned to Casper. "That's why I need you to look after it."

Casper blinked at him. From somewhere deep in the woods, a wolf howled. "Look after it?" Wow, he sounded inept, but the words just weren't landing.

"You know. Be the guy."

"The guy." Oh. Wait. "You mean, be you. Run the resort."

Darek nodded.

And he didn't know why, but suddenly the warm meal, the hour or two of escape peeled off him, and Casper's hand started to ache. In fact, every bone in his body seemed to scream. "No. Sorry, Dare. I can't."

"What—sure you can. Look at you. You're practically building your own home. You can fix the minor repairs on the cabins, chop the wood, and keep the place running. Maybe Raina could help on front desk—"

"No."

Darek stilled. "Really?"

Casper held up his hand. "If you hadn't noticed, I'm hardly a carpenter." He shook his head. "Trust me on this. I'm not you, Darek. I never have been, and I never will be."

"Casper—"

But he opened his door and slid into the seat. Blood pooled in his grip as he reached to close the door.

Darek hadn't moved, still just staring at him.

Casper shook his head. "You're the superman around here, not me. So please don't ask me again." Then he shut the door and pulled out, back to his tragedy on the hill.

4

D arek didn't know why his brother's words irked him so much. *You're the superman around here, not me. So please don't ask me again.* Once upon a time, he might have responded with a "That's right, bro." Especially since he and Casper always had a sort of rivalry going. But now, as he stood legs apart in front of an unsplit log, the twilight closing in on him, the glow of the woodshed spotlighting an hour's work, it gave him little satisfaction to send his axe down the center of the log, hearing it crack.

Feeling the power of a solid blow.

No, now, his brother's words only made him feel like a jerk, honestly, and he couldn't put his finger on why, either.

So chopping wood seemed the only option. Sweat had long ago soaked his back, turning his thermals itchy, and he'd shed his parka, down to his flannel shirt, despite the frigid air. He sunk the axe in the wooden block and tossed the two split pieces onto the growing log pile.

He probably had enough wood for the next two years of romantic campfires, but somehow chopping wood, the satisfying *thunk*, the burn in his arms and back and the sense of doing something—anything—felt better than going back inside to face, well...

How was he supposed to tell his parents—no, his father— that he was leaving them?

He set up another piece of wood. Took a breath. Raised the axe.

"Need any help?"

The question jerked him even as he brought down the axe. It bumped off the log, sent it flying.

Jace caught the piece of wood in one massive hand. "Whoa."

Darek wrenched the axe out of the chopping block. "Sorry. But you shouldn't sneak up on a guy wielding an axe."

"I only called twice from the stoop." Jace had pulled on his Blue Ox team parka, but left it unbuttoned and wore his fancy city boots. For a tough guy, he'd slicked up for his coaching job. "You okay?"

"Yeah," Darek said and reached for the log. "Just trying to get some work done before I have to spend the day tomorrow pretending to be Joseph."

Jace grinned. "Ah, the yearly live Nativity penance."

Darek set up the log. "Not sure why Ivy volunteered us." Actually, he wondered if it had something to do with family legacy. His parents had helped organize the living Nativity for years. Only recently had his mother let it go, and Ivy had picked up the mantle. Then again, that was before she knew she'd be abandoning Deep Haven.

No, not abandoning. Moving on to a better life. A life they both wanted—

"And so I said to her, maybe we need to get Darek and Tiger down to watch a couple Blue Ox games. Unless they'd rather visit the North Pole, you know, to see Santa."

He looked at Jace, who smiled. "So, you're back."

"Funny. Stand back." Darek sent the axe down, hitting his mark, splitting the log in one solid punch that cracked the night.

That's how it was done, thank you very much. He set the axe down.

"Wanna talk about it?"

Darek threw the wood into the pile. "Nope."

"Perfect. Me either. Need help?"

"Nope."

Jace had his jacket off, had gone over to the pile and picked up a handful of wood. Walked over to the woodshed and started to stack them.

Darek set up another log for chopping. "How's Eden's newest book?"

Jace returned for more wood. He was a big man—bigger than Darek by a couple inches, and once upon a time Darek had seen him take on two players at a time, as the Blue Ox enforcer. Funny, once he got to know Jace, Darek had discovered a compassionate, kind man. And no one supported his wife's career like Jace did.

"She's supposed to have a little East Coast tour in the spring when it comes out, but..." Jace picked up another armful.

Darek separated another log. "You have a full schedule."

"Something like that."

"Hard to choose, right? Between what your wife needs and your commitments."

Jace nodded, setting the logs. "And the good of the family."

Right. He'd been thinking about that. Tiger, and his friends here. But Duluth had a great hockey team, and maybe, in a bigger school, he'd really shine. Darek set up another log and wiped his hand across his brow.

A pale moon waxed down on it, turning it platinum. It brought up the memory, last winter, of Emmie's fall through the ice.

Jace had gone right in after her, without a thought.

"If you had to choose between the good of the family and the good of your wife, what would you do?"

Jace stopped, his arms full. Considered him. His breath crystallized in the air. "Could be the same thing."

Darek met his eyes. Nodded.

Jace turned away as Darek's axe cracked through the wood. Yes, it probably was. He threw the pieces onto the log pile. "I have to leave the resort."

The words made Jace glance over his shoulder.

"Ivy is getting appointed as a judge in Duluth. Three hours from here. It's not a daily drive. And I don't want her alone there."

"What does she want?"

"I can't take this from her. She deserves it."

"And you're hoping Casper can take over the resort for you." He retrieved another pile, stacked it.

Darek centered his last log. "*Was* hoping. He told me, well, that he wasn't me." The thought turned into a grunt as he swung the axe down. It got stuck in the middle and he worked to wrench it out.

"He's not," Jace said.

Darek wiggled it free. "He's capable of running this place."

"Sure he is. But...this place is yours, Darek. Yours and your parents."

And Jace had nailed it, hadn't he?

This place was his. And leaving it felt like...

He sent his axe into the log again. The pieces fell in two. He picked them up and held out the pieces to Jace.

Jace met his gaze. "Nothing worth having comes without a price."

"Thanks, coach." But he smiled.

Jace turned back to the pile. "So, you gotta tell your dad you're leaving."

"Yep. Merry Christmas." Darek set the axe into a log and picked up a load of wood.

Jace stacked his logs, then smacked off his hands. Stood in the cold, staring at the lake.

Darek considered him as he stacked the wood. "Could have ended differently."

"Yes. God is good." Jace sighed. "But all I can remember, really, is Eden screaming. It keeps me awake sometimes. I wake up in a cold sweat, thinking of how it could have gone differently."

Darek stared at him, a little nonplussed at his quiet confession.

Jace turned to Darek. "We're lucky men, to be given our lives, our wives, our second chances. I'll do anything to give my wife what she needs." He blew out a breath at that, as if he'd settled something, then reached for his parka. "Your parents ran this place for years without you. My guess is that they can figure it out." He pointed to the diminished log pile. "You okay here?"

"Yep."

"Good. Your mom's making cookies, and I like them hot." He started away, then turned. "But you know, hard news always goes down better with hot cookies and cold milk."

Darek laughed. "Right."

Jace headed to the house as Darek gathered up his last load. Jace was right. His dad might be getting older, but he could hire help, and...well, Ivy deserved the life she'd worked so hard for.

New seasons. He hadn't realized he wanted one.

He was stacking the last of the wood when lights turned into the drive, scraping across him. He held up his hand to shield his eyes. Probably Amelia and Grace, returning from the hospital.

Doors opened, closed, and the lights flicked off. He blinked to adjust his vision. "Hey! Everything okay at the hospital?"

He started toward the driveway, his feet crunching in the stiff, frozen grass.

"What? It's that bad? He's in the hospital?"

Male voice, familiar, and—what?

Darek's vision darkened, cleared, and— "Owen?"

His kid brother stood in the driveway, wearing a canvas jacket, a pair of work boots, an old wool hat, his blond hair long, like when he'd played hockey, staring at him with a look of horror.

"Yeah. Hey, Dare."

Darek walked over, wrapped him in a one-armed hug. "You came home for Christmas—wow."

"Yeah, well, after Amelia called me, I felt like I should."

"Right. Well, that's great of you. It'll mean a lot— Hey, Scotty."

Darek spotted Owen's wife, who came up beside Owen, then hugged Darek. She too wore work boots and a canvas jacket, her long dark hair in a braid.

She tucked her hand into Owen's. "Of course we're here. Family is important."

Owen looked at her, gave her a smile.

"Yeah, it is," Darek said. "But that's a long trip."

Owen frowned. "I know I live on the other side of the world, but I think maybe someone should have called me sooner."

Darek frowned. But yes, probably. He and Max had been teammates. "Sorry. I think we all panicked. I'm glad Amelia thought of it."

"I know I should have been home more often."

"It's fine. He'll be fine. Just hit his head. Mild concussion."

"Mild concussion? At his age? Sheesh." He shook his head.

"He's not that old, Owen."

Owen just stared at him.

Scotty tugged on his hand. "C'mon, O. Let's go inside. Talk to your mom. Then we can go to the hospital and see him."

Sheesh, now Darek felt like a bum. "Sorry. He's going to be fine. Really. Grace is with him, and mostly, it's about the long-term prognosis, not the fall he took on the ice. It was just a fluke accident. He's been doing really well lately, so he thought he was okay to play in the weekly pickup game. And then Tiger ran into him—"

Owen was staring at him. "He was playing *hockey?*"

"Yeah."

"Since when does Dad play hockey?"

Darek blinked at him. "Um...what?"

Probably, Owen matched his frown. "Amelia called and said that Dad was sick."

The words were a punch to Darek's sternum. He gaped at Owen.

"We got on the first plane out," Scotty said. "Please tell us we're not too late."

Too late? "How sick?"

Owen looked at Scotty, back to Darek. "You tell me. What is the prognosis?" He put his other hand over Scotty's.

Darek opened his mouth. Closed it. "I have no idea."

"What did the doctor say?"

"What doctor?"

"Darek, for the love of— The one at the *hospital.*"

"Maybe we should just go there now," Scotty said, pulling on Owen. "We'll talk to your dad and—"

"Dad's not at the hospital," Darek said. "He's here. But *Max* is. He fell on the ice. Hit his head. His Huntington's has gotten worse."

In the silence, as the night deepened around them, Darek could see Owen replaying their conversation too.

"Wait. Amelia called and said *Dad* was sick?"

"Yes," Owen said. "Is he?"

"I don't know." Darek raised a shoulder, a sort of fist around his heart. "He went to Mayo in October. But...I thought he was fine."

"Not according to Amelia," Scotty said. "She called and said that she overheard your parents talking, and...well, it's something serious. Something he doesn't want to tell you all until after Christmas."

Owen's mouth made a grim line. "So, we came home."

Wow. The sweat down Darek's back had dried, frozen, and now a chill whipped through him. "Right. Okay." He smiled at Owen. "Welcome back, bro. You need a haircut."

"And you need a bath."

Darek met Owen's grin. Then, sobered. "Not a word until after Christmas, then."

"Nope." Owen gave a nod, his smile also falling.

Then, behind Darek, the door opened. "Oh my—Owen, is that you?"

He turned and their mother stood on the stoop, her arms open. "Is that really you?"

Owen grinned. "It's not Christmas unless it's in Deep Haven. Or at least, that's what Scotty says." They headed for the door.

Darek, however, stood in the cold, in the darkness of the barren yard, a knot tightening in his gut.

Sorry, Ivy.

She knew it was a dream. Knew it because behind the images her brain was playing, in her semi-conscious state, Amelia could smell the vinyl of the recliner she sat in, hear a choir belting out "O Holy Night" in some faraway speakers, a chill slipping around her from the nearby window.

And none of it matched the smell of the savanna, the sounds of a Jeep's motor, the jar of the rutted road, the screams of Esther as she held her son in her arms.

She knew it wasn't real. Knew that it would end the same— with the boy dying in the middle of a dirty street. With her clutching Roark, weeping into his bloodied chest.

With another senseless tragedy in the war on Christians in

Nigeria.

"He's just a boy!" Esther's words, or maybe her own, as Esther held him, rocking, wailing. "Why?"

Why? *Why?*

"Ames. Wake up. Wake up."

She roused, near the surface of sleep, and frankly, she'd probably heard her own blubbering because she gasped, hard, the tears burning her cheeks.

Grace stood over her, holding a sub sandwich bag. "You okay?"

Amelia sat up, ran her hands over her cheeks. "Yeah. Just a dream—"

"A nightmare, from what it sounded like. I was about to get out of bed if you hadn't come in, Grace." Max sat in the bed across the room, clearly antsy, watching a hockey game on mute on the flat screen.

"Is Max right?" Grace asked. She set the bag on Max's tray. "Was it a nightmare?"

Grace shook her head. "It was a memory." She blew out a breath. "A bad memory."

Grace sank down on Max's bed, in the space next to him where he'd made a nest for her. Frankly, they'd all expected Max to be released by now, but they were waiting on a few tests. "What kind of memory?"

"The kind where twelve-year-old boys are attacked and left for dead while a bunch of terrorists burn down his father's church."

Even Max's eyes widened.

"Sorry. I just…" Amelia got up, shook her head. "Sorry. It still makes me so angry. His father was murdered about six months before that, and Kebe decided that he wanted to protect the church so he…he camped out with a machete, even though we told him to leave it alone. He was just…he was angry."

Grace nodded, as if she understood, but how could she? She

hadn't spent the past six years working in refugee camps in a half dozen Third World countries. Hadn't seen terror and hate capture young girls into slavery, kidnap young men, forcing them into war, separating families and...well, evil seemed to be winning.

Amelia walked to the window. Max had the lights off in the room, and in the semi-darkness she could see Main Street Deep Haven twinkling, the posts lit up in festive cheer. Oh, that everyone could grow up in the safety of Deep Haven. Amelia felt almost embarrassed at her secluded, perfect childhood.

"He was there when a group of Boko Haram showed up and decided to torch the church. He tried to stop them and was shot."

She wrapped her arms around herself. "Roark was there. He was nearly shot, too, pulling him away. We drove Kebe to the nearest city, but...he died on the way."

"Oh, Ames," Grace said. "I'm so sorry."

She lifted a shoulder. "I didn't want to say anything. Ree and Seth were so excited about their wedding, I didn't want to wreck it. And then afterwards, well, I was trying to put it behind me."

Grace got up, came over to her, and slipped her arms around her waist. "I know what helpless and frustrated feels like. You can talk to me."

Right. Amelia leaned her head back against her sister. "I know."

Grace said nothing.

"Roark is angry at me for not setting a date."

"Oh. I see." Grace turned her around. "But you can't get Kebe out of your head."

"Maybe. I don't know. I just...our last conversation got cut off. And I keep thinking about him, there, and what could be happening."

"Call him." Max's voice from behind them. Grace let her go

and she turned. Max had found a sandwich in the bag. "You should call him. In the absence of conversation, the mind plays tricks." He looked at Grace. "It's better to talk things out. Even if it's on a sketchy connection."

Grace drew in a breath, looked away.

She didn't know what was going on between them—but it couldn't be easy to manage a terminal disease. Maybe they needed a moment.

More, yes, Max was probably right.

She checked her watch. Midnight, Nigerian time. But he would probably welcome a call from her, at any hour.

She hoped.

"I'll be right back." She headed out the door.

Grace followed her out. "Ames?"

Amelia turned. Grace held her jacket and purse. "A Holly Jolly Christmas" played softly in the hallway. "Yes?"

"I think you need to go home. I…" Grace looked away. "I need to talk to Max about something. And he's not going to like it. And there's going to be a fight, and…well, and I'd very much appreciate it if you also told Yulia that I'm spending the night here."

Oh. "You two okay?"

Grace gave her a thin-lipped nod. "We will be. For at least a while."

A rock formed in Amelia's throat. "I'm so sorry you're going through this."

"Don't be sorry. I signed up to love Max, in sickness and health. For better or worse. This just happens to be one of those worse moments. But Max is worth all of it." She reached out and touched Amelia's arm, squeezed. "Just like Roark is. He's okay, Amelia. Roark is tough and smart and you two are a great pair. Marry the guy already." She winked.

Amelia managed a tight grin. "Yeah." She took her jacket. "See you at church tomorrow?"

"Maybe." Grace gave her a hug. "Tell Mom to save us some cookies."

Amelia headed out of the hospital, through the lobby, into the night. Winter always turned the sky dark early this far north, and stars cascaded across the deep velvet sky. For a moment she imagined Roark in their village, in the cement house he shared with one of the other single pastors. He always walked her to her house, every night, under a dark, star-strewn sky.

And every night, she turned to him, put her hands on his amazing chest, lifted her face, and kissed him with everything inside her.

Oh, she loved him. His husky voice, with his sexy accent, the smell of him, that dark hair that she loved to twirl between her fingers, the way he wrapped her in those strong arms...yes, she longed to be his wife.

Marry the guy already.

Yes. Fine. Okay.

What was her problem that every time she clamped onto a yes, something akin to a boulder settled in her chest and cut off her breathing?

It was just like when she lived in Prague and came home, her tail tucked between her legs.

Fear. At least she could name it now. Fear, but also...dread.

And that's what she couldn't figure out.

She walked out to her mother's car and got in, turning it on, waiting for the heat to kick on. Oh, they needed snow to temper this frigid blast.

She pulled out her phone. Roark was top on her list of favorites, and she pressed his number, setting the phone to her ear.

Yes, she just needed to hear his voice. To know he was okay. That he still loved her. And maybe, yes, she'd push through it all and set a date.

The call went through, rang.

He might be sleeping, and she hated waking his roommate, Jayamma, but Roark often got calls from overseas, at all hours, from his trust fund manager.

Rang again. *C'mon, Roark.*

Again.

She closed her eyes against a rush of images. Their village in flames, the men shot, their bodies left in the mud. Roark, at gunpoint, taken because he was a Westerner. Or worse, fighting them, because he was Roark and— *Stop!* She was just tired, and overreacting to the memories and—

It rang again. And again.

And *again.*

Finally, it flipped to voicemail, and oh, she was pathetic because she leaned into the planes of his tenor. "Hey, Mate. Leave me a voice and I'll give you a bell back. Ta!"

"It's me. I miss you. And, yeah, I know. It's time. Call me back, or as you would say, give me a bell." She smiled, ended the call.

Then she set the phone on the seat and turned on the heat. She was pulling out when it vibrated in the darkness. Stopping in the empty lot, she picked it up.

"Roark?"

"No, Miss Amelia, it's Jayamma. I got your call. Roark no be here."

She stilled, her ear making out his deeply accented words. "What? Where is he?"

"He left two days ago. Visited a church, I think. He no tell me where."

He left and... "He didn't tell you where he was going? And he didn't take his phone?"

"He left in the night. Before I wake. I don't know. I'm sorry. I will tell him you called when he be back."

Don't panic. He was fine. His phone didn't work in the bush,

69

so often he took a radio. In the morning, she'd call Esther and see if she'd heard from him. But he'd be *fine*. Roark was a survivor—from a very early age when his family was killed on vacation. He'd survived that tragedy, and so many more over the past six years.

Really. He'd be... Just. Fine.

"Thank you, Jayamma," she said softly.

"Merry Christmas, Miss Amelia."

"Merry Christmas," she said as he hung up, her eyes on the stars, listening to her heartbeat against the stone that filled her chest.

Wow, he'd missed this. Owen hadn't realized how much until he walked into his childhood home and the season swept him up with the cinnamony and chocolate scent of his mother's fresh-baked cookies, mixed with the lingering scent of pot roast, and the tall home-cut fir tree that filled the two-story space of the great room.

It soared, filled with ornaments and twinkle lights, the stockings hung on the banister while a fire crackled in the hearth. And to top it off, of course, Dean Martin was singing "Let It Snow!"

Yes, please.

Sunny, his mother's golden retriever, ran up to him, and nearly knocked him over, slathering him with kisses.

"Hey, buddy. Hi." He barely knew the dog—hadn't seen it since it was pup, but then again, this was the greeting everyone got at the Christiansen's.

His mother rescued him, coming in behind him with Scotty, shooing Sunny away.

"Owen!" his father came into the room and Owen nearly moaned with the strange feeling that swept through him as his

70

father pulled him into a hug. "What a great surprise!" He held him away. "I thought you'd be in the Bering Strait, catching crab."

"Actually—"

"Owen! What—?" Eden came down the stairs, her eyes bright with the old joy at seeing him. She'd been his biggest fan —even traveled to Minneapolis to live with him in his years of junior hockey and then his rookie season of the Blue Ox.

He owed her too much to count.

Now she wrapped her arms around his neck as his father embraced Scotty. "You are a sight for sore eyes, number thirty-three."

The years when the regret and loss over his hockey career pierced his heart had passed and now he simply grinned into her old nickname. She let him go. "What brings you home?"

Oh. She didn't know. He glanced over her shoulder, to where Darek stood in the entry. Darek gave a tiny shake of his head, and Owen said easily, "Scotty suggested we come home for the holidays."

Maybe he wouldn't mention the boat wreck quite yet. Wait for that moment when it seemed right to tell them how they'd nearly died, again.

So, maybe never.

"Are you hungry? We have a few leftovers," his mother said. She'd held him for a very, very long time, and a few tears still clung to her eyelashes. She was getting older—lines around her mouth and eyes—but still had the enthusiasm for her kids that, frankly, he wished he could pass on.

But he'd made promises to the woman he loved.

"We ate in Duluth. But I can never turn down a cookie."

"Uncle Owen?"

He turned and spotted Yulia at the top of the stairs. Max and Grace's daughter—whoa, now twelve, maybe—her hair in a long tawny braid down her back, wearing a pair of leggings and an oversized sweatshirt. "I didn't know you were coming for Christmas."

"Apparently, none of us did," said a voice that Owen knew too well. Of course Jace, Eden's husband and his former teammate, would be here. Jace had come out of another room upstairs—and now followed Yulia down the stairs.

Yulia gave him a quick hug, then turned to her grandma. "The girls all want you to read us a story."

"Of course," his mother said. "Cookies are on the cutting board. I expect to see some when I return."

"Ha," he said as Jace took his hand, shook it.

"What's that about?"

"Oh, once Mom made cookies and I managed to finish them off in about ten minutes, while she was upstairs doing something. Actually, it was me and Casper and Darek—we were playing a game at the table, and she thought we'd put them away."

Darek came in. "Ate forty-eight cookies without even realizing it, between us. No regrets."

Owen laughed. Yes, he missed this.

Scotty had wandered over to stand in front of the tree. "Wow. I've never seen a tree this tall. I mean, *inside* the house."

He walked over. "It used to be a family tradition to cut down our own tree from our property. That was before the fire, of course, but we'd fight over what tree we loved. Eden always won."

"Did not, you big baby." She stood over another table, where puzzle pieces were scattered, peering over her options. "You just can't admit that your trees were always duds." She looked over at him, and grinned, all teeth.

"Oh, the stockings! I remember these." Scotty had walked over to the stairs, where the family stockings, each one crafted by his mother, hung on the banister. She reached out and touched one. "This one has my name on it."

"That's because Ingrid always lives in the hope you'll be here," his dad said. "It's nice she'll be able to fill it this year instead of sending a package."

"Dad!" Eden said and glanced at Tiger. "Santa fills them!"

"Seriously, Aunt Eden?" he said, glancing up from his phone.

"What are you doing?" Owen said, coming over to sit beside him. Wow, the kid had grown. What was he—fourteen?

He was, of course, playing some hockey game on his phone. "How goes the hockey?"

"He's fantastic," Darek said. "Has the Owen Christiansen touch. He really belongs at a bigger school, so scouts can see him."

Huh. That was a sentiment he'd never thought he'd hear from Darek, the hometown boy. Except, once upon a time, Darek had left, following his dream of being a hot shot. But he'd returned.

Just like Owen should have. At least, more often. No, every year. But Scotty didn't like fussing over holidays. Usually, they spent Christmas on the boat.

Yeah, it wasn't super.

This. This was super.

And by the look on Scotty's face, she agreed. Or he thought so until she wiped her cheek.

What—?

"Ivy left earlier, with Raina," Darek said. "Joy and Layla are in the Christmas pageant tomorrow at church."

The names hit him, and he looked at Scotty. Right. Layla. His biological daughter, now adopted by Casper. They never really talked about her.

No, they *never* talked about her. He'd buried his curiosity about her in his heart, releasing her to Casper. Even when Casper sent the occasional text and update, he'd kept it to himself.

He hadn't deserved her, not really. And, in truth, wasn't her dad.

Just her biological father, the guy who'd slept with her mother, Raina, in an act of selfishness on a night they'd all like to forget. But that was the *other* Owen. The "before Owen" who was angry, broken, and wounded.

And angry and broken and wounded people broke and wounded other people.

But everything had changed when Jesus reached down and simply saved his dark soul from himself and...well, this Owen was grateful for every redeemed moment he got.

"We'll see them at church," he said, meeting Scotty's gaze. "We might have brought gifts from Uncle Owen and Aunt Scotty."

She smiled. See, everything was fine. He'd made peace with it all. Moreover, he planned on being the very cool uncle. The one with the eye patch.

The one that sailed the high seas.

"I should get our bag," Owen said and got up.

"I'll help," his dad said, and walked to the door.

"Me too," Darek said, and Owen shot him a look. What, did he think he'd take the old man out back and wrangle the truth from him?

"It's just a duffel bag. We travel light. I'll be right back." Owen slipped on his boots, grabbed his jacket, and headed outside.

The air was clear, the stars bright, and for a moment he was back on the boat, watching the northern lights arc over the polar cap, across the dark waters.

He didn't miss it. The boat, the sea, the cold.

The worry.

The thought reached down and wrapped around him.

No. That wasn't right. That was their life. He was just weirdly homesick.

Walking out to the rental, he popped the trunk and was

reaching for their oversized duffel bag when light splashed over him. He shaded his eyes, and a Ford Escape pulled up next to him.

The door opened. "Owen! What—you made it!" Amelia leaped out of the car and into his arms.

Oh, she'd grown up. As in a beautiful, redheaded, twenty-six-year-old woman. It struck him silent for a moment.

He met her eyes. "I talked to Darek. He didn't know about Dad. But we agreed not to say anything to him until after Christmas."

She clung to his jacket, and her eyes almost looked wet.

"You okay?"

She blinked hard. "Yeah. Yes. I'm fine. And good. I agree—we don't want to wreck Christmas. How long are you staying?"

Not long enough. "Just until the New Year."

"Perfect. Long enough for me to beat you in a game of Speed Scrabble."

He laughed as he picked up the duffel and followed her into the house. Scotty was sitting at the table, working the puzzle.

His mother came down the stairs. "You can put that in the den, Owen. I'll make up your bed."

"No, I can do it, Mom."

She came over, kissed his cheek. "I'm so happy you're here." Then she stepped back, taking his hand, glancing at Scotty. "I'm just wondering when I'll get to read a book to one of your children." She raised an eyebrow.

Scotty had turned, and now her eyes fixed on him.

Oh.

But he couldn't say it. *We're not having kids.* The words just stuck, right there in his throat.

So, like an idiot, he gave a sort of strange, feeble laugh, cleared his throat and said, "You'll be the first to know, Mom."

Then, without looking at Scotty, he fled to the den.

5

Really, Grace should be heading back to her home, the beautiful log home she and Max had built, overlooking the mighty Lake Superior. The one decorated with pictures they'd taken of Cancun while on their honeymoon, and of course, his den of promotional posters and epic shots of his hockey career. The one with family pictures of her, Yulia, and Max, taken in Disney, and on a camping trip in the BWCA, and that epic, crazy white-water rafting trip down the Colorado River where she'd never screamed more in her life.

Wow, Max had changed her world, swept her out of her small, quiet life and made her believe that she could live larger, with him. He'd made her believe she could be strong, courageous, and bold.

What a lie.

She pulled into the quiet driveway of the Evergreen Resort, Max's voice still thundering in her head. *It's time for us to stop living in denial.*

He hadn't shouted it. It wasn't Max's way. No, the thunder

was from the impact, the fact that he'd...well, he'd already given up.

Her jaw tightened before another wash of tears could burn through the steel resolve she'd managed on the drive up. *Hope is not denial!*

Her words, but they landed on his steel-edged, almost barren expression. And she knew.

It was over.

She wasn't sure how their conversation had gone so south, so quickly. Or maybe it was destined to fail because the moment she walked back into the room after Amelia had left, Max had picked up the remote and turned off the game and said, quietly, "I know what you're doing."

That had stopped her cold.

"I know the tests I agreed to—the extra blood drawn, the MRI brain scan, the meeting with the neurologist—are about the trial."

She came in and sat in the chair Amelia had just vacated.

"Then you'll do it?"

He drew in a breath, offered the tiniest, sad smile, then shook his head.

Admittedly, she came apart on the inside then, her heart— maybe even her soul—shattering into so many ragged-edged pieces.

"Listen, I know you're freaked out about the procedure. I get it—but I talked to the doctor, and they give you this drug that makes you forget—"

"It's not that. I'm not afraid of getting my skull opened, Grace. C'mon—I risked that every game on the ice." His voice had turned a little clipped.

Maybe hers too. "Then why not?" She stood up. "Why not? If it works, it could extend your life. Our life. Keep our family together."

"And if it doesn't, I die that much sooner, in agony. And I

wouldn't even care about that if it didn't also mean that I will have to spend months in Rochester, away from Yulia and you." His eyes had darkened, and he looked away.

"I'm not going anywhere but by your side. And I can home-school Yulia—"

"No!" He looked back at her. "She loves school—"

"She loves you!"

She stared at him, not caring that tears dripped off her chin. "Don't you see what you're ripping away from us? Not school. Not time. Hope, Max. You're ripping away hope."

And then he said it. The words that were sitting in his soul. "It's time for us to stop living in denial." He met her eyes. Didn't blink.

"Hope is not denial," she said softly.

"Hope is for the weak," he responded, just as quietly. "I am not weak. And I refuse to be impaired or broken or away from my family." He swallowed, drew in a breath. "We knew this would happen, Grace." He reached out for her.

And she...well, she stepped away.

Stepped *away*.

The poor man lay there, his hand outstretched, and she just couldn't take it. Couldn't walk with him into this place of darkness.

And then, oh no, she'd called him a coward. She winced at her words, still pinging in her head. "What—so I want to explore all the avenues to keep you alive. That makes me weak? I think that makes you a coward!"

Even now, sitting in the car, in the quiet of her parents' driveway, she couldn't believe herself.

Or his final words, the flash in his eyes, the way he folded his hands across his chest, or his deep, calm, always-Max tone. "Don't mistake acceptance for fear, Grace."

Oh.

Right.

And it occurred to her, with his words, that maybe *she* was the coward.

And to prove it, where had she driven? Back to her childhood home.

Because, you know, tragedy couldn't find her here.

She turned off the car and got out. The wind whispered through the trees, stiff and cracking. Without the grace of snow, the world was dark, brittle and harsh, but overhead, the stars glittered down.

The lodge door groaned as she opened it, but she kept the light off. Clearly everyone was in bed, but the hood light remained over the stove and she spotted plates of cookies covered in plastic wrap. The tree also glittered, with red and white lights that played against the dark windowpanes.

Shedding her coat and boots, she tiptoed into the great room, grabbed a knitted afghan, and settled onto the sofa. The fire had almost died, just embers left, glowing now and again, fighting for life.

"Gracie?"

She looked up at the low voice and spotted her mother coming down the stairs, tying the belt on her robe. "Is everything okay?"

Sunny had trotted down in front of her mother and now jumped up on the couch, wedging in next to Grace. She folded her hands into her beautiful golden fur. "I didn't want to go home."

Her mother sat down beside her and pulled her into a hug. "I get it. There's always room for you here."

She knew that, but she burst into stupid tears anyway.

Her mother said nothing, just rubbed her back.

"I'm sorry—"

"Shh." Her mom handed her a tissue, and she wiped her eyes.

"I tried to get him into a trial he didn't want to be in. And now he's mad at me."

"If I know Max, he won't stay mad long. He's the most patient man I've ever met."

And that just made her want to cry again. "I know. He's patient and understanding, and he lives life for every moment and...I just want more of those with him."

"That is complete understandable. But that's not the real problem here."

She stared at her mother. "It isn't?"

"No. The real problem is that you're not sure how you're going to get through all this, are you?"

Oh. It was as if her mother had reached in, found the hidden shard that had embedded inside, and pulled. The pain swept over her, and she gasped, then pressed her hands over her mouth to stave off the shout inside.

Yes.

"Oh, Grace." Her mother pulled her close again. "You're not alone."

She nodded, wordless. No, she wasn't. She had her parents and Yulia and her siblings—

"God has not forsaken you or Max. And He never will. It's just that you've never had to need Him this much."

She pulled back, and her mother handed her another tissue. "We look ahead and we see thin air. Or, maybe massive waves. And we're asked to get out of the boat and walk on water, and that sounds preposterous."

"You're going to tell me to keep my eyes on Jesus, right?"

"Actually, I'm going to remind you that when you're sinking, Jesus will not let you drown. He will catch you. He will hold you, even when the world is coming apart around you."

"Max has no hope. He says it's for the weak. He says that he's accepted his fate."

"I'm sure he has. But you can't tell me that he's not afraid. Hope takes immense courage. It is for the brave, and for the bold. Because what is hope but faith that we aren't abandoned?

80

That there is a better end to the story than we can see? That all of this has a good purpose? Hope is the one thing that we have to give when the world is at its darkest. And right now, Max is in his personal midnight."

"He says I'm in denial."

"I'm not saying that God will choose to heal Max. I'm saying that perhaps there is a bigger story here, and that is the hope you need to help Max see."

"I don't think I know how to do that."

"Well," her mother said, getting up. She reached for another afghan. "'Blessed are the poor in spirit, for theirs is the kingdom of heaven.' You don't need to come up with the answer, Grace. God already has." She tucked the afghan around Grace, then leaned down and kissed her forehead. "Just wait for it."

She turned off the vent light on her way back upstairs.

Sunny stayed curled up on the sofa. Grace petted her, staring at the tree, the decades of gathered ornaments, the tree lights splashing red against the window. Took a breath.

Show me the story, Lord. Show me the story.

In the early press of dawn, Raina was hiding it, but Casper knew she was crying.

He'd thought she was better, but then again, they never really talked about it. Not that he didn't care, but really...mostly he felt relief.

Raina, on the other hand, grieved. And he hadn't a clue how to fix it.

"Raina?" Casper rolled over in their warm bed, the one he had been hating to leave to return to the stupid money-pit house, and slipped an arm around her. "You okay?"

"Mmhmm," she said, but it came in hiccups and shoot, not even a little bit. He pulled her against him, her back to him.

Outside, the wind banged against their ancient windowpane—maybe he should have spent money on replacing the fifty-year-old windows in the house they'd purchased in town, but he'd poured all his money into renovations. He'd also funded the kids' college funds, and put away enough for their retirement, but a part of him didn't want to invest in a house that wouldn't be their forever home.

Which was the problem, really. They were always in wait mode. First, it was wait to get married, until he could find Owen and tell him that he'd fathered a child and ask him if he would allow Casper to adopt her. And then there was that whole murder charge thing, and finally the wedding, and then they'd been trying to have another child and finally Rhett had come along, and all the time he'd been working on the house, and then…

"I miss him too," he said quietly.

She drew in a breath. "It could have been another girl. Now, we'll never…"

"I know."

Her voice hiccupped. "Sorry. I thought I was okay."

She smelled good. Her flannel pajamas, the cream she slathered on her skin at night. And under their blankets, despite the nip in the air, they were warm and cozy and…

He kissed her neck.

She stilled.

He sighed.

She rolled over onto her back, met his gaze. He ran a thumb across her cheek. "I love you."

"I love you too," she whispered, and her gaze fell to his mouth, then back.

And she smiled. Nodded.

Oh. And suddenly his hand didn't hurt, and the small hole inside his heart seemed less vacant. He bent his head to kiss her, the taste of her so familiar, so perfect, so…his.

So what if they couldn't have more children. This was enough. She was enough. Their family was enough—

"Mommy! Wake up! We have to get ready for the pageant!"

Perfect. They'd forgotten to lock the door. Casper rolled away before Layla could ask any questions and caught her just as she jumped on the bed.

"I'm going to be an angel!"

"Of course you are!" He tossed her onto the bed between them and tickled her as Raina slipped out of bed and reached for her robe. She looked over at him.

"Sorry, champ."

Yeah, well, like he said, this life was enough.

Layla wiggled away from him and ran out after her mother. He heard Raina getting Rhett up as he closed the door and then hopped in the shower.

By the time he emerged and pulled on his jeans and a sweatshirt, his was mind on the mudding waiting for him at the house. The smells of bacon and eggs lured him downstairs where he found Raina in the kitchen, Rhett on her hip, her hair up, singing "Away in a Manger" with Layla who'd already donned her angel costume.

And that's when he realized what he'd done.

Raina looked up from the pan of eggs and just stared at him. Layla stopped singing, her arms still folded together, forming a manger. "Daddy. Are you going to work?"

He'd put on his jeans without thinking, really. Now, he stared at his clothes and back at Layla, and her eyes filled. "Are you not coming to my pageant?"

Raina's mouth pinched at the edges.

Aw....

Casper hit his knees. "Sorry, baby. Yes, I am. Daddy just got a little confused." He glanced at Raina who was shaking her head. "I can't wait to see you sing."

Layla brightened up.

Casper kissed the top of her head, then shot a look at Raina. "Sorry."

She raised an eyebrow.

"What?"

"I'm just waiting for a but..."

He made a face. "I do have a lot of work at the house. I probably need to duck out of Sunday dinner at my parents' place."

"Casp—"

"Raina, if you want this house to be done by Christmas eve—which, mind you, is six days away—I'm going to have to miss some things!"

Oh. He hadn't meant to shout.

Raina's gaze went to Layla.

He hardly ever shouted, but lately, all he seemed to want to do was shout. To hit something, to...run.

Yes, that was it. He was itching to just leave. To go *find* something. To pore over lost maps and legends and unearth something priceless.

And then maybe he wouldn't be a guy stuck in a small town, working at a kayak rental place, hanging drywall in his free time, trying not to miss dinner, or tuck-ins or Christmas pageants, and most of all, not the guy who let his wife down, over and over and over.

He wanted to be the guy he'd been when he'd married her, an unmarried single mom, and he'd been her hero, the guy who fixed things.

Raina was still staring at him, her eyes thick. Behind her, the eggs were popping in the grease. "I hate that stupid house."

He blinked at her. "What—?"

"It's consumed you—for years really, but especially since..." She swallowed. "Since we lost..." She sighed and put Rhett down. He crawled across the kitchen, already an adventurer.

Raina turned off the heat, moved the pan away. "I hope you like your eggs well done."

"I don't care about the eggs." He stepped up to her, put his hands over her shoulders. "What did you say?"

She sighed. "Nothing."

"What do you mean you hate the house?"

She drew in a breath, still not looking at him. "I don't hate the house. I just..." Turning, she smiled and pressed her hands to his chest. "Just go upstairs and change, okay?"

He stared at her, those beautiful brown eyes that trusted him. Needed him to keep his promises. Believed in him, especially when he'd been accused of murder.

He'd do anything for her. "Okay." He kissed her forehead.

Anything.

Even if it meant pretending that everything was okay.

He sighed and headed up the stairs. Church, then the house.

Because despite what she'd said, he'd made a promise. And he planned to keep it.

He changed, and by the time he came back down, she had plates set. He ate with the children while she changed, and they headed off to church.

They had to park at the far edge of the lot, and the children were already lining up as they entered. Layla ran off when she spotted her Inga, holding the wire halo Raina had made for her, those dark braids piled up on her head.

His mother pulled up her grandchild in a hug as Casper walked over.

"Hey," she said, letting Layla go. "You okay? You left in a rush last night."

"Yeah," he said, and couldn't help but cast a look over at Darek, his words rushing back. *Be the guy.*

Okay, he'd been a little rough on his brother. But he'd been hurting, and tired, and maybe a little peeved because Darek had it so *easy*. Well, now, at least. Casper wasn't so thick as to not remember the years when he'd been a single dad. But now he had Ivy and a son and a beautiful daughter, and his wife was going to be a judge, and he'd managed to pull the Evergreen Resort back from ruin after the forest fire decimated it so long ago, and frankly, he *was* a superhero.

And Casper was, again, just trying to keep up.

Wow, maybe he needed to go back to bed, get up on the right side...

Or just stay.

And then...and then he nearly did head for the door. Because even as he looked over at Darek—dressed, of course, in costume as Joseph—and Ivy, as Mary, helping line up the kids, Darek was talking to a man with his back to Casper. And recognition clicked in.

Wait.

No. What—?

Owen was back?

He stood, mute even as Raina came over, Rhett on her hip, wearing a tiny man suit.

Right then, Owen turned. His gaze fell on Casper.

For a moment, everything cast between them. Their epic fight, over seven years ago now, and then, of course, the moment when he found Owen, two years later, fresh out of the ocean depths, cheating death, in a hospital room in Alaska. And he could hardly forget the look on Owen's face when Casper told him that he had a child, or the taste of fear, unlocked from deep in Casper's heart that Owen might try and woo that child, and his mother, away from him.

"Casper!"

But he hadn't, and in fact had allowed Casper to adopt her, and hadn't once tried to suggest that he had any claim on her, and shoot, but Casper was just tired and edgy and...

Owen pulled him into an embrace. "I missed you, brother!"

It shook him free. "Owen." He embraced him back. "I didn't know you were coming home."

Owen looked good. Sure, he still had the eye patch, but

captaining his own crab fishing boat on the high seas had turned him burly, a little more solid, and he even had a maturity about him as he pulled away and smiled at Casper.

"Spur of the moment idea from my wife." He reached out and took Scotty's hand. One would never know that this petite woman not only helmed a fishing boat but had also worked as a detective. In fact, she'd saved him from a life in prison.

"Hey, Scotty."

She hugged him. "Good to see you, Casper." She stepped back and glanced at Raina. "And you, Raina."

Somehow the two women had made peace with the past too.

See, everyone was just fine. Calm down, Casper.

"Was that Layla coming in with you?" Owen turned, looked at the kiddos lined up. "Wow, she's grown."

Casper swallowed. "She's seven."

"Yeah, I know." Owen turned back to him. Met his eyes, gave him a nod, a sort of close-lipped smile.

Casper met it. "She's an amazing kid."

"I'm sure she is. She has a great dad." Then he put his arm around Scotty. "It's been a while since we've been in an actual church. It's nice."

Hmm.

Well, okay then.

He followed them into the sanctuary, behind Raina who followed his parents into their row, second from the front, on the right.

They filled that row up, then the next, with Darek and Ivy behind them, and Jace and Eden and the kiddos, and even Grace and Yulia, and a part of him settled into place when they rose and sang "Joy to the World."

Yes. For right now. This was enough.

Frankly, Eden didn't know how Mary did it.

Nine months pregnant, on a donkey for fifty miles, in labor. Giving birth in a barn. Eden wasn't a fool. She'd been in labor. Had three babies.

There was no way Mary looked as good as Ivy made her out to be as she and Darek took their places in the living Nativity, as their choir of cherub angels, including Layla and Joy, sang "Silent Night."

No way she was that calm, that at peace, that...trusting. *Let it be to me according to your word.*

Yeah, Eden wasn't even close to Mary because, well...

Well because Mace still had syrup on his face from this morning's breakfast, and Sully had taken off the tie that Jace had put on him and wrapped it around his hand like it might be boxing rags, and Emmie was kicking the back of the pew, even as Jace sat, his long arm around all of them, grinning at the silly pageant on stage.

Eden clamped a hand on Emmie's knee and shot a look at Jace. He glanced at her and frowned, and she nodded at Sully, who had started to air punch, Rocky style.

Jace leaned up and pulled Sully onto his lap, shutting the future MMA champ down.

Her greatest hope was that they'd manage not to break any ornaments, no one would fall into the lake, and, well...maybe she'd figure out how to face a baby she hadn't expected.

Not unlike, well, Mary.

Let it be to me according to your word.

The angels finished their song, and the crowd clapped as the children filed off the stage. Pastor Dan, older, probably wiser, got up and thanked the parents who'd helped, made a comment about Darek being a good likeness of Joseph, to which he got a few chuckles.

Her stomach picked then to churn, and a wave of nausea hit her. Perfect. Please, don't let her throw up in the pew.

And now she was sweaty.

She looked at Jace, who sat between her and the edge of the side row. Climbing over him was like trying to dodge a linebacker. But going out the center aisle from their oh-so-favorite place at the front of the church...

Not happening.

"Welcome back to so many familiar faces," Pastor Dan was saying. He pointed out Eli and Noelle Hueston, home from Florida to see their kids, and Colleen's brother, Jason, was home from some movie he had a role in out in Hollywood.

"And the Christiansens are warming up two entire pews. Great to see you back. And Owen, all the way from Alaska."

Eden could smile at that. Sweet Owen, who'd finally found his way back to peace. She wanted to get him alone and find out, really, how he was doing, but he and Scotty had gone to bed early after their long flight from Alaska.

Oh, wow, she really might be sick. She drew in a long breath. Another.

"I just want to say a few words before we close the service."

No, c'mon, Pastor—

"We forget sometimes, in the telling of the story, what exactly this event means for the world. For eternity."

No, she didn't. She got it. Salvation. Eternity. Hope—

"Emmanuel."

Oh.

"God with us. We often focus on the truth of salvation as the purpose of His coming but let us not forget that Jesus walked this earth for thirty-three years as a human."

Nope. She got up, hunched over and practically hurdled Jace and Sully, and he had to move to the side and put Sully down and even caught her hand as she shoved past him. But she shook her head, and then put her head down and practically fled the sanctuary.

She made it to the bathroom, slammed into a stall, hit her

knees and lost the one pancake she'd gobbled on the way out the door.

Perfect. This was just...perfect. Sitting on the tiled public bathroom floor, sweaty, her stomach lurching, and...

She couldn't do this. Couldn't—

"Eden?"

She leaned against the wall, on the floor. "In here, Mom."

Her mother's face appeared below the door. Eden gave a feeble wave, then kicked the door open—she hadn't bothered to latch it. "It's a party."

Her mother opened the door. "Honey, are you okay? Food poisoning?"

Eden made a face.

"Oh." Her mother looked her over, her brow raised. "I see. How far along are you?"

"Fourteen weeks."

"Really." Her mother sat on the floor too. "And you're still sick?"

Eden lifted a shoulder. And then, weirdly her eyes filled, and she just shook her head, looking away. "I don't know, Mom. I just...I don't know."

"What don't you know?" Her hand slipped over Eden's.

"It's..." She closed her eyes, unable to say the words.

"Honey."

"We had a test." She pressed her hand to her eyes. "The baby has a severe heart problem. And maybe Down syndrome."

Silence. And then her mother squeezed her hand. "It's going to be—"

"I don't want it, Mom." Had she really said that? She took her hand away, looked at her mom. "I don't... Wow, I'm a terrible person. A terrible mother. How can I ever think that—of course, I want it. It's our child, but..." Her voice broke. "I can barely keep up with the kids I have. The twins—they strip everything out of me, and Emmie...I keep thinking of last year, the ice—"

"We were there, and she is fine—"

"But what if we weren't? And now, even if the baby lives, I'll have a child with special needs and what if...oh, Mom, what if I'm not enough? What if something terrible happens and—"

"Eden." Her mother caught her face. "Eden. Breathe. Just breathe."

Eden swallowed. "How did you do it? Six kids, Mom. *Six*—"

"I sat in the bathroom and cried a lot."

She stared at her. Her mother didn't smile. "You're not kidding."

"Sometimes I brought a pillow with me so I could scream into it."

And then she smiled.

And Eden didn't know whether to sob or laugh. "Seriously?"

"It was better than strangling Casper, right?"

Eden laughed. "Right. I guess."

"I suppose the jury is still out on that one."

Eden leaned her head back against the tile. Sighed. "I'm scared, Mom. I've been trying not to hear the doctor's words for two days now, ever since she suggested that we end the pregnancy, and the very fact that I...that I keep thinking about it—really. Mom. What kind of person am I?"

"Eden. Be real. You and I both know you'd never end the life of your child."

She drew in a breath. Met her mother's eyes. Nodded.

"Feel better?"

"Yes. But...I still...I'm so tired, Mom. And I don't know why, but I feel so alone. Jace is...he's such a great husband, but he's been so weirdly cheerful, as if he hasn't a clue what this means for us." She shook her head. "I guess it doesn't change anything for him, really, but I had plans, you know? I had a book tour in the works for my next novel, and the boys just stopped wetting their beds at night and I was getting my life back..."

"This is your life, Eden. Ordinary moments where you get to

train up amazing children. Yes, your career matters, and God will make a way for that, I know it. But you've been given a great responsibility—and yes, not to be cliche, a gift—and—"

"'Let it be to me according to your word.'"

"What?"

"It's what Mary said to God after Gabriel told her she'd have a baby."

"And do you remember what he said before he told her that?"

"Um. Don't be afraid?"

"Yes, but even before that… 'The Lord is with you.'" Her mother took her hand. "Emmanuel. You have no idea how God will be with you…but cast yourself to the moment where Mary had her baby, and it might have been in a manger, but God *still* provided."

God with us.

"Hey. You guys okay?" Amelia pushed open the bathroom door. Behind her, the sound of "The First Noel" filtered into the room. "Oh. Are we crying? Why are we crying?" She came over and sat down next to her mother.

"We're talking about what happens when you feel like life is too overwhelming," her mother said.

Amelia sighed, looking at Eden. "Yeah, I get that. Like when your fiancé wants to set a date and you sort of think that maybe the world is imploding and getting married isn't such a great idea—" Her eyes widened. "Sorry. I just couldn't hold it in anymore."

Eden looked at her mother, back to Amelia. "You're in the right place."

Amelia sighed. "I just…I came home thinking I'm ready, and last night, when I talked to Grace, I thought maybe I was, but…"

"Everybody okay?" Ivy ducked into the room, still wearing her Mary attire. "Why are we on the floor?"

Scotty had come in behind her. "Church is on the last hymn, so I'd give you about five minutes, max, of alone time."

"We're having a discussion about why Amelia doesn't want to get married," Eden said.

"Wow," Amelia said. "Way to throw me under the bus." She looked at Eden. "Really?"

"I'm a journalist. I like to get to the facts." She made a face. "Sorry."

"You don't want to get married?" Ivy sank down on the floor too, pulling up her dress. "Why not?"

"I do—I just..." She sighed. "About a month ago, my friend's son was murdered, and ever since then—no, before that... I just keep thinking about how life can go so wrong, and how maybe it's better to just not go there. Like Scotty and Owen not having kids yet. Maybe it's just better if they don't, right?"

As soon as she said that, Eden's gaze went to Scotty, who stared at Amelia, her eyes wide.

And then, just like that, Scotty burst into tears.

Well, wasn't this fun.

6

E ven to her own ears, Amelia sounded like a jerk. It was better if Scotty and Owen didn't have kids? Sheesh, who says that?

And to make it worse, Scotty sat on the bathroom floor, her hands over her face, *crying.*

Tough, beautiful Scotty, a former cop, boat captain—

Wow. Even Eden was looking at her like she might be a villain. What did they expect? Amelia had spent most of the night awake in a room filled with seven-year-olds, on her old bed, staring at the ceiling, seeing visions of Roark, shot, or being tortured, so, yeah, maybe she'd lost a little control of her mouth. "Scotty! I'm so sorry—! I don't know why I said that. I didn't mean it. Of course you'll have kids."

Scotty only shook her head.

Oh boy. Outside the bathroom, the sound of voices suggested that their cry fest might be interrupted, soon.

"Scotty, honey. What's going on?" Her mother of course, with the right words. "Is this about my comment? I'm so sorry— you and Owen take all the time you want. In fact, if you never have kids, then, that's okay—"

"We nearly died!" She looked up, something almost wild, horrified in her eyes. "We nearly died, *again.*"

And for a moment, her words shut the room down and probably everyone went to the horrible story of Owen and Scotty being swept overboard in the raging Bering Sea, how Owen nearly perished with a punctured lung, and their terrifying hours in a flimsy lifeboat.

"What happened?" her mother said softly.

"Exactly what you're thinking," Scotty said, looking at her, hard. "Our boat...a weld broke and water got into the void between the hulls and we...we nearly went down." She exhaled hard, as if she'd been holding that in for a while. "Owen risked his life trying to weld it shut. Crazy. He hung over the side of the boat, and sure he was clipped in, but I thought any minute, the ocean would grab him. But he was so determined to save the boat and yeah, he bought us a couple hours, but..." She blew out another breath. "We nearly went down with the ship."

"Oh, Scotty. How terrifying."

She nodded. "I never thought I'd say this...but I think I'm done."

Done? Amelia exchanged a look with Eden.

"Done?" Ivy said. "Done fishing for crab?"

"Mmhmm. But I don't think Owen is. He met with the insurance guy, and of course they'll cover it, so he got Carpie to pull it into his shop to fix it. He wants to go back out as soon as we get home."

Her mother's mouth had formed a thin line, but she nodded. Amelia never knew how her mother took it, watching Owen push himself over and over again into trouble, first in hockey, and then, hopping on a motorcycle and disappearing for years as he tried to figure out how to make sense of his life. Sure, he'd lost an eye in a fluke accident, but really, he'd lost himself too, turning into a guy nobody liked. And then, one day, he showed up redeemed, the Owen that no one expected.

Except, he'd returned to the sea, and with it, probably revived their mother's fervent prayers for a different kind of salvation.

"It's the life we told ourselves we wanted," Scotty said quietly. She wore a pair of clean black yoga pants and an oversized white sweater. "But..."

"But you don't want it anymore."

"I don't know what I want. I love what we have—I love working with him. He's an amazing fisherman, and captain. He knows how to handle the boat, and frankly, everybody loves him." She sighed. "And it's all we have."

Again, Amelia shared a look with Eden. Then Eden turned to Scotty. "What do you mean? I mean, you guys are young and—"

"Owen doesn't want kids."

And now Amelia just wanted to crawl from the room. Yep, she won the jerk award for the day. Maybe the entire season.

"Why not?"

"Our life isn't exactly built for kids. And, I...well, I told him once that I probably wouldn't make a good mother—"

"What? You'd be a *great* mother," Ivy said.

"I wasn't raised with a mom. I really don't know how to be one. My dad...well, remember, he was the original fishing boat captain. But I think Owen probably agrees with me. He's never brought it up again."

"Honey." Her mother reached out and took Scotty's hand. "Have you talked to him about it?"

Scotty shook her head. "I don't know how. He's so excited about fixing the boat and..." She looked at Amelia. "I get it. Your life can go south fast, and why bother setting yourself up for all that tragedy and pain."

Amelia nodded. Thank you.

"Except, you miss out on all the happy parts, too, right?" Eden said. She looked at her mother. "Ordinary moments. Like when Jace and I see the boys do something funny and we know they're just mini versions of us. Or even, I don't know, when I tuck the kids in bed and the house is quiet and they're asleep and Jace and I stand in the doorway, exhausted, holding hands, knowing that life, in that moment, is perfect. Ordinary moments that add up to an extraordinary life."

Amelia stared at her.

She and Roark didn't have ordinary moments. Well, okay, maybe when he walked her home at night. And those times when she'd looked up from teaching a refugee to read and seen Roark staring at her from across the room. His smile, even from twenty feet away, could send a hot ripple through her entire body.

Okay, yes, maybe the urge to marry him could overshadow the what-ifs. Even make them bearable.

"I like that," Scotty said. "Like when we're both up early, drinking coffee, watching the sun rise from the eastern shoreline, fire across the sea, knowing it's going to be a great crabbing day. Or when he comes in from the deck, sweaty and salty and yet still wraps his arms around me and calls me Captain, my Captain." She looked up. "Maybe that was too much information."

"Amelia, close your ears," Eden said. "Unless you're reconsidering that marriage thing."

She laughed. Eden grinned at her.

"Yes. Probably, except..." And then suddenly, it all swooped in over her. "Roark is missing."

"What?" her mother said.

"I called him last night, and he didn't pick up. And then his roommate called back and said he'd left two days ago...but didn't take his phone. Which he never does, unless he's going into the bush, but I called Esther this morning, and he didn't take a radio either and no one knows where he is and..." And

saying it all out loud had suddenly made it real. "What if...
See..."

"Stop," Scotty said, her hand on Amelia's. "I don't know
Roark very well, but I heard about him from Owen, who heard
about him from Darek and Casper. Apparently, this guy crossed
an ocean to find you and actually learned how to be a lumberjack in order to win your heart, so... I'm thinking that he's
pretty tough, even if he is a Brit."

"He's actually American, but...yeah, he's got a sexy English
accent." She looked at Eden. "I said it. Sexy."

Eden laughed, and Amelia let Scotty's words sink in. A little.

He did know how to take care of himself. And he wasn't a
twelve-year-old boy. But it wouldn't be the first time an American had been taken by the Boko Haram and...

"What is going on in here?" Grace stuck her head into the
bathroom. "Since when do we get to leave church in the middle
of the service? Can I just remind you that we sit in the second
row? The entire congregation thinks someone died, or, well, I
don't know. Eden—why did you leave church?"

Eden glanced at her mother, then Grace. "Morning sickness."

Grace's mouth opened.

"Seriously?" Amelia said.

Eden glanced at Scotty. "Yes."

"Congratulations." Scotty touched her hand. "Really."

"Wow, Eden. Congratulations." Grace walked all the way in
and embraced her sister as Eden got off the floor.

Ivy, too, hugged her. "This is so exciting!"

A knock came at the door, and Grace frowned, then turned
to open it.

Darek stood there. "Um, I need Mary."

"Right. Sorry, Joe," Ivy said and headed toward the door.

"And, by the way, Amelia, you might want to get out here."

Amelia followed Ivy out. "Why?"

And then her world simply stopped as Darek pointed, as she

followed his gesture all the way to the foyer where her brothers stood around a man, shaking his hand, clapping him on the back.

Dark hair, mussed, and long enough for her to twirl her fingers into. Unshaven, wearing a pair of cargo pants, boots, a canvas jacket, and looking fresh out of the bush.

Coming halfway around the world to find her.

Roark.

He looked over, met her eyes. But he didn't smile.

In fact, if she knew him right, she might even pinpoint his look as...fury?

Darek would bet that Joseph wasn't freezing his backside off, sitting in a barn on that *O Holy Night* in Bethlehem. Darek couldn't feel his nose, and really, who had birthed this stupid idea for humans to stand out in frigid weather, pretending to be the holy family while children petted sheep and goats? Never mind that no one wanted their real baby to be in the cold, so his lovely wife held a doll in her arms.

He should be at the resort, doing the puzzle, or helping set the table as their family gathered for Sunday dinner. He could almost taste the ham, the sweet potatoes, his mother's rolls—

"Can we go?"

Ivy sat on a hay bale near him, her blue costume over a massive parka, her hands covered in mittens as she ducked her nose into a scarf that the first Mary had most definitely not worn. In fact, he'd remembered Ivy giving birth, and probably Mary wasn't super excited about having a ragtag group of smelly shepherds tromping all over her privacy. "Not yet. We still have kids here."

Tiger and local author Joe Michaels were supervising a few of the lingering kids who wanted to press their cold hands into the thick weave of sheep or pet the bony head of a goat. Even Tiger looked chilled to the bone, his hands shoved deep into his pockets, shoulders hunched, his booted feet stamping.

Darek's gaze went to Gabe, Joe's brother, who crouched beside Sully, helping him pet a goat. Jace stood nearby, chatting with Joe.

Maybe it was a gift that came with his Down syndrome, but Gabe had a tender heart for both kids and animals and had helped run the petting zoo for years.

Tiger looked at Darek, with something akin to pleading in his eyes. *Rescue me.*

He supposed it wasn't unlike so many looks he'd given his father over the years, when he'd been in over his head—like after Felicity, his first wife, died and he'd been left alone to raise Tiger. His parents had come to his rescue again and again and...

And shoot, but he couldn't leave them to run the resort alone. He'd made promises to them too. Except, his father didn't seem sick. Not even remotely hampered. He'd caught him carrying both Eden's rug rats after church under his arms, like a couple of footballs.

If his dad was sick, he was hiding it well. But Amelia wouldn't ask Owen to come home without a good reason.

Still, something didn't feel right, and here Darek was, the cold turning his fingers stiff as he held the silly staff, wondering what to do.

So maybe he was a little like Joseph, because certainly he'd felt he was in over his head, what with being the earthly father to the Son of God. Talk about responsibility. But he had walked away from his world when his wife needed him, when he discovered there was danger stalking them, so there was that.

"I'm calling it," Darek said, standing up. "We need to get to the house. I don't want to miss dinner. And I need to talk to my dad."

Ivy shivered. "We need to wait until all the kids leave."

"I'm sure, at some point, Joseph told the shepherds to take a walk."

"Darek, just a few more minutes. Look at Claire and Jensen's daughter. She's such a doll."

"Fine. I just…" He looked at Ivy. "Owen told me that my dad is sick."

Ivy broke her pose to look at him. "What?"

"Yeah. That's why he came home. Because Amelia heard Mom and Dad talking about not wanting to tell us something. And you know he went to the Mayo in October."

"He said everything was fine."

"Yeah, but you know my dad. He doesn't like to worry anyone." He glanced over to Tiger. Finally, the Atwoods were leaving. He lifted a hand to Jensen. "If it was something small, he would have mentioned it to me. No. This is serious, Ivy."

"You need to talk to him."

"Yes, I do. Okay, we're out of here." He stepped out of the nativity set and walked over to Tiago, one of the young shepherds, who was looking at his phone.

"Shift's over, T. Go home."

"Thanks Mr. C." Tiago lived just down the block and took off across the barren, crunchy grass.

Darek waved at Tiger, gave him a cut sign with a hand across his chin.

"Wow. Joseph might need to check his crabby meter," said Ivy as she also said goodbye to another shepherd.

"I'm not crabby. I'm just concerned."

Ivy held open the church door for Darek as he headed inside. "Me too. And, did you see the weirdness between Amelia and Roark. I wonder if he knows."

He'd have to call Lena, the town vet, and ask her to pick up the animals. "Knows what?"

Ivy pulled off her blue dress. "That Amelia is having second thoughts about getting married? And I know she gave him a big hug and kiss, but he didn't look real happy to see her."

"Aw, he'd just traveled across the ocean. He's probably tired." Darek worked the stupid Joseph costume off his head. "Why doesn't she want to get married?" Although, they'd been engaged for nearly six years, which felt, yes, troublesome.

"She says that she's seen too much tragedy—and it didn't help that Owen and Scotty nearly died on a fishing trip. Again."

He looked up from where he was texting Lena. "What? How?"

Ivy was folding their costumes. "I don't know. Their boat sprung a leak or something. Anyway, Scotty said she doesn't want to go back out to sea, but Owen does, so... I think she wants to start a family."

Really.

"Darek. What are you thinking?" She put the costumes in a box and gave him a look.

"Just that...maybe Casper was the wrong person to ask to take over the resort. Maybe Owen's homecoming is providential." And then, too, he wouldn't have to confront his father. Maybe it was God working this all out so he didn't have to be the bad guy.

Just like God had for Joseph when He appeared to him in a dream and told him to escape to Egypt. Maybe he should let God be a little more in charge of his life's skirmishes.

"I'm hungry," Tiger said as he came in. "Lena is outside getting the animals, so I think we can go."

The truck didn't warm up until they had practically pulled into the Evergreen driveway. They got out and Darek's stomach growled as he walked in, the smells of dinner a reminder that he hadn't eaten breakfast.

"Daddy!" Joy ran over. She still wore her halo from today's pageant. She launched herself into his arms. "We're nearly done with the puzzle."

He put her down and glanced over to see a quiet group working the puzzle. Amelia stood near Roark, who had clearly showered, his black hair wet and a little curly, wearing a clean pair of jeans and a thermal shirt that looked familiar. Maybe pillaged out of the Christiansen boys' leftover clothing.

Roark seemed intent on discovering a specific piece.

Ivy was right. Trouble in Roar-melia-ville.

His father stood in the kitchen, holding a pair of hot pads, reaching in to retrieve the ham from the oven. "Ten minutes, and we'll be ready to eat."

Eden mashed potatoes on the stove, his mother stirring gravy.

He did a quick survey of the room. Owen and Scotty were also at work on the puzzle, while Jace sat on the sofa and watched a hockey game, the television on silent. Looked like a rerun of a recent Colorado Blades game. Frank Sinatra singing "It Came Upon the Midnight Clear" played on his parents' speakers.

The rascals were on the floor, working on Legos, but Joy returned to the puzzle, alongside Layla.

"Where's Grace?"

"Max has been discharged," his mother said, pulling out a couple hot pads for the table. "She went to get him. They'll be here soon."

Raina stood at the window, Rhett on her hip, and a glance outside showed Casper playing with Sunny in the yard, throwing a stick for him.

Darek walked over. "That looks fun."

"He wants a dog. Maybe after we get the house done." She lifted a shoulder, glanced at him. "Are you frozen to the bone?"

"Just about." He should probably let his brother off the hook —no doubt their conversation was bothering Casper too. Darek opened the sliding door and stepped out onto the deck in his bare feet and flannel shirt. He was already cold, so it didn't really matter.

The sun barely bled through the thick, shadowed clouds, and it all sent a dour pallor upon the thin ice of the lake. How he wished it would snow.

"Hey!"

Casper turned from where he was wrestling a stick from Sunny. She jumped back and wagged her tail, barking. He threw the stick into the yard and walked over to Darek. "Hey."

"So. Um." Darek shoved his hands into his pockets. Okay, maybe he should have grabbed a coat. "I just wanted to let you know that I get it."

Casper blew on his bare hands. "Get what?"

"I know you're super busy, and you didn't sign on to run the resort and...sorry I put that on you."

Casper looked at him, blinking.

"Yes, this is me apologizing."

A smile tweaked his brother's face. "Yeah, well, me too. I shouldn't have said that you're a superhero."

"Why not? I am." Darek grinned.

Casper shook his head. "Right. So, what are you going to do about the resort?"

Sunny had run back and now dropped the stick at Casper's feet. Darek picked it up and tossed it out again. From behind him, the sliding door opened.

"I'm going to ask Owen."

"Ask me what?" Owen came out, also shoeless, no jacket. He closed the door behind him.

Darek took a breath. "Ask you to stay. To run the resort."

Maybe he'd spoken in French, or Russian, because Owen just stared at him.

"Did you hear—"

"Why would you need me to run the resort?"

"Because Ivy's been appointed to a judgeship in Duluth and...well, we're moving."

Owen blew out a breath, then clasped both hands behind his neck. "Wow, man. I wish I could."

Sunny came running up to the deck with the stick, and Owen walked over, crouching in front of the dog, petting him as he dropped the stick.

He picked it up and shot it back out into the yard. "I got a boat in the shop and a crab fishing business I've put on hold... But more, this isn't the life my wife wants."

Darek just stared at him. "Yeah, well, things change, Owen. I mean, my wife wants to be a judge. And she's worked hard for it. She's earned it and I don't want to stand in her way."

"I get that, Darek, but—"

"No, you don't get it. I already broke the heart of my first wife—I can't do that to Ivy. She, and her happiness, is everything to me."

He didn't know where that came from, but apparently, Owen had his own lit fires because—

"And Scotty is everything to me! We've built a life there—"

"What kind of life, Owen? You don't have a family, or kids. You have a boat. And a crew that changes every year, and a dangerous job that freaks us all out and—don't be so stinkin' selfish."

Everyone went quiet.

Okay. Whoops. The words had come out before he could stop them. "Sorry. I don't know why I said that—"

"Wow. And, really?" Owen said, and Darek could practically see the ruff rise on the back of his neck. Darek might be bigger, but Owen had spent years on the ice, learning how to fight. But Owen put his hands into his pockets, clearly not the guy he'd been. Still, he leveled a look at Darek, his voice low and sharp. "Who here set the bar on selfishness, Darek? I remember the day you accused Felicity of purposely getting pregnant—"

"This isn't about that," Darek said softly.

"Isn't it?" Owen's eye flashed. "Guilt over being a jerk of a husband the first time around—"

"Owen," Casper said.

"I'm not doing that to Scotty." Owen looked at Casper, took a breath. "I'm calm, so just step back."

Casper held up his hands in surrender.

Darek's jaw tightened. "I agree...I was a jerk to Felicity. And I am trying to be a good husband here. Do you seriously think I want to move away, to raise my kids in a city? Where we have to walk to a local park, or worse, reserve ice time to shoot the puck around? We grew up in the never never land of the north —do you seriously think I don't want to give Tiger and Joy exactly that? But Ivy wants this, and I love her, and I'm not going to be the jerk who says no!"

"And I'm not going to be the jerk who tells Scotty that she has to abandon her life. She grew up on the sea, and frankly, she doesn't want this life."

Sunny had run back, dropped his stick, and now barked at the trio.

Owen scooped up the stick and threw it with all his strength. Then he rounded on Darek. "Listen. Truth is, I miss this place. I miss this world. I don't love spending every minute at sea, and I really don't like the very real possibility that some day we end up at the bottom of the Bering Sea, but Scotty doesn't want to be a mom. And yes, that just about takes me apart, especially when I see all you guys with your amazing families."

He walked out to the edge of the deck, faced the lake. "More than anything I'd like to be a father. And in a perfect world...I might even say yes, Darek." He turned, faced Darek. "But this isn't a perfect world. It's the world we signed up for. And I, for one, am grateful for it. So..." He held up his hand. "I'm sorry, bro. And I know you're not a jerk anymore, just to be clear. But...I can't take over the resort."

He met Darek's gaze, his chest rising and falling, then looked away, shaking his head.

Casper raised an eyebrow, made a face.

And what was Darek going to do? "I get it, Owen. Maybe we just have to face the truth..." He blew out a breath. "Maybe it's time to sell the Evergreen Resort."

Owen's jaw tightened, but he looked at Darek and nodded.

Casper looked away, ran a hand over his mouth.

"So, um, I guess I missed all the fun?"

The voice behind Darek made him turn, and Max stood in the open sliding glass door.

And behind him, Ivy was staring at him, something of pain on her face.

"Your mom told me to tell you that it's time for lunch."

There used to be a day when he and his brothers fought for the last piece of ham.

Now, never had Owen seen more pitiful eaters.

He wasn't sure what Scotty had heard, because she gave him a strange look as he and Darek and Casper filed inside, after giving Max a hug. But Ivy wasn't looking at Darek, and she deliberately put Tiger between them when they sat down.

And they weren't the only couple acting weird. Jace had pulled out Eden's chair for her and she told him she knew how to seat herself. Which had Jace frowning, and then Grace and Max sat opposite each other, and Max kept looking at her, something of concern on his face, but Grace was all about helping Raina cut up food for Layla. And then there was Amelia, who kept looking at Roark with a half-smile, only to be met by a tight-lipped, grim nod.

Over it all, his mother talked about the pageant and how cute Layla and Joy had been, with a nod toward Tiger and the live Nativity, which might be a tally in the Never Move Back column.

Except Owen had meant it—not just about wanting to be a father, because, technically, he already was, sort of, but...

Yes, he'd like to stay here. Not only to watch Layla grow up, but because he wanted the life he'd seen everyone else enjoying. For years, he felt like he stood on the sidelines looking in, watching a life that would never be his.

Because hockey had taken up all the room in his life.

"Owen, more ham?" His mother held out the tray.

"Sure. It's delicious, Mom."

A few hums around the table, as if his siblings latched onto his words.

"So good, Mom," Darek said.

"I could never cook a ham like you," said Eden.

"I love the glaze, Mom. You'll have to give me the recipe," added Grace.

"I haven't had ham since...well, goat, yes, but ham isn't a huge favorite in Nigeria," Amelia said, glancing at Roark, who had looked up and smiled at his not-mother-in-law, nodding.

"I took it out of a bag and slapped it into the pan. There was a glaze packet attached," his mother said, raising an eyebrow.

"It was still good," Grace said. "Especially after hospital food. Right, Max?"

"Mmhmm."

Max looked a little wan, and definitely thinner than Owen had remembered, and Owen well remembered the day when Max had been more than a teammate, but a friend.

And then, of course, the fight happened, and with it, the accident that ended his career. But he and Max had made peace. Or at least he thought they had, except Max's gaze had gone to his eye patch and he'd winced.

He wanted to say, "Hey, it's no big deal," but that would only make it obvious, so he ignored it. Besides, as far as raw deals went, Max won the prize.

"Are you going to play in the New Year's game, Uncle Max?" Tiger asked.

Ivy shot him a look and Darek drew in a breath. Beside Owen, Grace had also tensed.

"I dunno. Maybe." Max looked at Owen. "If Uncle Owen does."

"Uncle Owen plays hockey?" Sully asked.

"Sure does," Jace said.

"I thought he was a pirate," Mace said.

Owen looked at him and crooked a finger. "I am. Arrgh."

Mace laughed, and so did Sully, and a few chuckles went around the table. Even Layla laughed, putting her hand over her mouth. "You're so funny, Uncle Owen."

Oh wow. A streak of heat went through him, and suddenly he couldn't move, couldn't breathe.

His ham stuck in his throat, and then he swallowed, and it went down the wrong way. And in a second, he was coughing.

"Owen!" Scotty said, even as he turned away from the table and kept coughing. This was fun.

"I'm fine," he said, holding up a hand. He picked up a glass of water. Drank it down.

Everyone was staring.

"Really. I do know how to chew my food. Usually. Mom, have I mentioned how good the ham is?"

A few smiles returned, and his dad turned to Roark with a question about Nigeria.

So, yes, Owen would like to stay, and sure, maybe a small part of that was about Layla.

Seeing her breezing into the church today with Casper and Raina, it sort of knocked him back. Seven years old, with long dark hair, but wow, his blue eyes.

He hadn't expected that. And his nose, too, and perhaps even a bit of his wild side, because she'd hiked up her angel costume to jump from riser to riser on the stage before the service started.

But he'd handled it without his heart thumping through his chest. She didn't belong to him, and he knew it. And was okay with that. Really.

Just like he was okay with his promises to Scotty.

"We work with a small school inside a refugee camp from the north. They've been run out of their villages because of the Boko Haram, and we work to help them resettle in the south, or be reunited with families," Roark said.

"Sounds dangerous," Jace said.

Eden gave him a tight-lipped shake of her head, and Jace frowned, but Roark didn't seem to notice.

"It is. Can be. We work with small churches in some of the danger spots, and we've seen more than one congregation attacked. But it's important work, helping people in crisis…"

Owen looked at Amelia, who was staring at him. She nodded, then plastered on a smile.

Huh. He knew his little sister the least, but it seemed, even to him, that she wanted to run from the table.

Maybe that's what the weird huddle in the bathroom had been all about today. One second Scotty was sitting beside him, the next, she'd slipped out of the pew. He hadn't really noticed, frankly, his attention on Pastor Dan and his sermon.

His words about how Emmanuel didn't just save them once, but came to be here, to save them every day.

Like He had, again, as the *Wilhelmina 2* took on water. As Owen had tried everything to patch the hole that would sink them.

Sort of felt like his life, once upon a time.

"I'm sorry, Mom, but I gotta run." Casper put his fork down. "I still have a lot of work to do at the house." He leaned over to kiss Raina, but she looked away, and he only got her chin.

Oops.

And he wasn't the only one who saw it. Out of the corner of his eye, Owen spotted his father's quick, but distinct, frown. Then the expression of concern as Casper got up, kissed his mother's cheek, and headed for the door.

Yeah, Owen had seen that look before. When he'd woken up from surgery after the terrible accident that had derailed his life for a while. Not just concern, but a bone-deep worry.

"Need any help?" Owen said.

Casper was already at the door. "I dunno. Can you mud and tape drywall?"

Owen was up. "If I can weld a ship in the middle of the night in high seas, I think I can figure out how to mud and tape." He glanced at Scotty, and she was giving him another strange look. But he got a smile.

And that was fire to whatever urge had him on his feet. "I'll see you guys later," he said and headed out the door after Casper.

Casper was waiting by his truck. "You're seriously going to help me drywall my house?"

Owen had pulled on his jacket and now added a hat and gloves. "It's getting weird in there."

Casper grinned, opened the door. "Yeah. Not sure what's going on, but between Jace's over-kill niceness, Ivy's killer attorney looks at Darek, and the cool front between Roark and Amelia, I'm running for my life."

Owen didn't mention the cluster bomb of the missed kiss between him and Raina. Talk about a minefield.

He got in, and Casper pulled out.

"I noticed the duct tape on your hand. What happened?"

"Nail gun."

"Ouch."

"Not my best moment."

They turned onto the road into town. Overhead, the sky had

turned a pale gray, thick with clouds. Maybe, hopefully, snow crept their direction.

"I can't believe Darek is leaving," Owen said.

"He didn't mean it, you know. About you being selfish." Casper glanced over at him. "He's just stressed out."

"I get it. And once upon a time, I was pretty selfish. But now, really, it's about Scotty."

"She really doesn't want kids?"

"She told me once that she wouldn't make a good mom. And that probably we shouldn't bring any kids into our lifestyle."

Casper turned on the dirt back road that Owen guessed would lead to his house, outside town. "First, Scotty was probably just talking out of fear. I remember Raina freaking out about being a good mom before Layla was born."

Owen nodded, glad that Casper didn't mention the uncomfortable season where he was dating the woman that Owen had slept with. Forgiveness. Redemption. It made for new seasons.

"Layla is perfect, Casper."

Casper drew in a breath.

"You're doing a great job with her."

He nodded his head, slowly. "Thanks."

And ever so briefly, like a heartbeat, Owen felt it.

Regret.

Maybe Casper felt it too, because he looked at him. "Owen, I—"

"She's your kid, Casper. I know that."

"But if you don't have any more children..."

"Still your kid. And you heard her. I'm her cool Uncle Owen."

"It's the eye patch."

"It's my amazing humor and general awesomeness."

Casper grinned, shook his head. "And, he's back."

Owen laughed.

Casper sighed. "You know, Owen, someday we will tell her. And if you want to be more in her life—"

"No. And I'm fine with keeping the secret until you think she's ready. Listen...I got myself in over my head, and you stepped in. Thank you."

Casper glanced over. "No. Thank you. Layla is a treasure."

And now it got awkward in the car. Owen stared out the window. Ahead, he could see the old Wilder home. A beautiful Victorian, with a porch that ran around the perimeter, and a turret that overlooked the lake. The perfect place for a couple little girls to grow up.

"You know, about your lifestyle. I know you like the sea, Owen, but—"

"I don't like the sea. I get seasick, and it's cold, and I hate the boat—there's no privacy, and I am so sick of seafood, and—"

"You sound like you used to when you would come home from practice and whine about the coaches or practice, or the way the trainers taped you up..."

"I did? Wow. I loved hockey."

"I know." Casper glanced at Owen. "I'm no different. I think whenever we feel overwhelmed, we can suddenly hate our lives. Like this stupid house. I made Raina a promise that we'd be in it by Christmas, and I've been busting my back to get it done, so much that I despise the place." He took a breath. "It was almost done, and then the bathroom shower fixture was left on and flooded the place. The ceiling came down into the living room."

"You have all the fun."

"Yeah, well, there are days when I just want to keep driving. Somewhere. Anywhere."

Owen nodded. "I used to whine. You used to talk about the places you'd go, the treasures you'd find. I don't think I have anything to whine about anymore."

"And I've already found my treasure."

"Wow. That was really sappy."

"Blood loss." Casper held up his hand.

"I'm going to need to keep away from that nail gun."

"Did you really hang over the edge of your boat, welding in the middle of high seas?"

"Yep."

"Oh boy. You sure you didn't get hit harder on the head during your hockey days?"

"Not even a little," Owen said, laughing.

melia consoled herself with the fact that Roark wouldn't have traveled halfway across the world to see her if he didn't still love her.

Right?

But he was acting capital W, weird, even after she'd launched herself into his arms. Even after she'd kissed him right there in the church lobby, in front of her entire family and the church family.

And he'd kissed her back, although it felt almost...sad. Or maybe it was simply longing and he'd had to, of course, throttle back.

He'd been throttling back for six years, really, and it had started to show, recently, with his ardor waning, as if he couldn't pour his heart into something that might only get them into trouble.

But she'd tasted something else this time.

Yes, she'd name it sadness, and it had occurred to her during dinner that maybe something terrible had happened. Something he couldn't tell her over the phone.

She'd tried to take his hand, weave her fingers through his at least twice, but he hadn't responded.

Yes, something was terribly, devastatingly wrong. And after Owen and Casper left, she just about leaped up from the table to drag Roark out of the house to the open-air conference room that was the deck.

Although, it wasn't the most private of places, at least not with the sliding door ajar. Poor Owen. Darek's final words had bled through the glass into the main room and she winced when Owen said Scotty didn't want to be a mom.

Especially after what Scotty had said in the bathroom.

Another capital W, weird.

"Dessert, anyone?" her mother asked as she cleared the plates. "I have cookies."

"None for me," Eden said, and Scotty too shook her head.

Amelia might have wanted some, but her stomach could barely hold the ham and potatoes.

"Me!" Layla said, and so did Tiger and the other kids and her mom got up to retrieve the plate.

"I think I'm going to head over to Casper's place after lunch. I'm wondering if he needs some help," her father said.

Amelia didn't miss the look of relief on Raina's face.

"I'll go, too, Dad," said Darek.

"And me, if that's okay, Eden," Jace said, glancing at his wife. She nodded.

"Amelia, I need to talk to you," Roark said quietly in her ear, as if reading her mind.

She looked at him and nodded. They stood up just as Max said, "I'll go too."

They escaped to the entryway as Grace responded with an, "Are you kidding me?"

"C'mon. It's going to get sparky in here," Amelia said and handed him a parka. She donned her own and closed the door behind them.

"Why?" Roark said, zipping up his jacket.

"Because Max just got out of the hospital."

"What happened?" They walked over to Darek's chopping block. Usually, his chopped wood was left in a pile for days, but now only wood chips littered the ground where he threw the logs. Instead, they were piled neatly in the woodshed.

"Remember when you learned to chop wood?"

"I also learned how to saw a log," Roark said. "I did it to show you I could fit into your world." He made a face. "Silly."

"I didn't think it was silly."

He nodded, then looked around. The sun had made it to the backside of the day, although still high. His breath crystallized, and she could almost see him churning through his thoughts. "The place looks good. Darek has worked hard."

"And the forest is coming back." Darek had planted a massive line of fir trees that stood almost eight feet tall. It cordoned off the resort from the scrub brush, pine, and poplar that grew up around their property.

"So much growth in seven years." He drew in his breath. "I would have thought we might see the same."

She frowned. "What?"

He gave her a smile, and it was just as devastating as the day he'd shown up at her house, having followed her home from Europe, to tell her he loved her.

"Darling, we need to talk."

Clearly.

"I was really worried about you," she said, stepping up to him and touching his coat. "I called you yesterday, and Jayamma picked up your phone. Said you'd been gone two days and hadn't taken your phone."

"I left right after our call."

Oh.

"I think my phone might have fallen out of my pack, because I didn't know it was gone until I got to the airport."

He went silent again, his jaw tightening, and he even closed his eyes as if in pain.

He'd left after their call. "Everyone is okay at the school."

It was sort of a question but became a statement when he nodded. "They're fine."

"And so...you jumped on a plane because..." She stepped in front of him, searching now for his gaze. He finally met hers. Oh, he had beautiful eyes. So blue that sometimes she just lost herself in them.

Now they darkened. "I'm sorry, Amelia..."

Oh. No— She backed up. "Are you here to *break up* with me?" She could barely get the words past her fisted chest. "Roark?"

"I didn't want to do it over text."

She blinked at him. He had the courage not to look away, but simply flattened his mouth, drew in a breath.

"No. Roark—"

"I just had this feeling you weren't coming back. You've already been here two weeks longer than you planned, and I kept telling myself it was because you and your mum might be planning a wedding, but...no. You haven't even set a date. Again." He cocked his head. "Or have you?"

She shook her head. "But—"

"No, darling. Listen. I am not going to coerce you into marrying me. The first few years I understood it. You were young, you wanted to wait. I didn't mind. I wanted you to be sure. And then, of course, we traveled a lot, and I understood your need for us to get to a less chaotic time. But in the last two years, well, I've started to see the truth."

"No—"

"I just couldn't understand why you keep putting me off, and it came to me that I've wasted six years waiting for you to love me."

"I do love you!"

"Just not enough to marry me, luv."

He spoke softly, not cruelly, not brutally, but it still had the effect of a blade to her heart. She stared at him, shaking her head, her eyes blurring. "I do—"

"Seven years. And you still can't set a date—"

"My dad is dying!"

She didn't know where that came from—desperation, maybe, and it worked.

He drew back, a look of horror on his face. Opened his mouth.

"I just found out. And I don't know for sure, but...something isn't right. And he doesn't want to tell us. I overheard them talking—remember, I told you."

Except, had she? She couldn't remember.

His chest rose and fell, and then he turned away, running his hand across his mouth, as if thinking.

"I promise, I'll set a date. As soon as I know...as soon as..." She swallowed, and he turned, his mouth set in a sad, thin line.

"No. I'm sorry about your father, Ames, I really am. And I know that you're scared."

Tears burned down her cheeks. "I am scared. I'm scared all the time, Roark. Kebe—"

"Kebe died. And I agree, it was terrible. But we don't have to stop our lives because of the tragedy of others."

"How can you even think about being happy when—when terrorists are kidnapping little girls and shooting little boys and—"

"And families are murdered right in front of you?" His eyes were hard in hers.

Yes.

Right.

His voice gentled. "Life doesn't have to be perfect to be happy. Sometimes you have to find the happy places between the pain." He cupped her face in his hands. "That's what we have, Ames. Happy, between the pain. Or...it's what I thought we had."

"We... I love you, Roark."

"I know. And I love you too. But life is scary. And it will always be scary. And you can't stop that by not marrying me."

"I *know* that."

"So then what's the problem?"

She stared at him, not sure how to voice it. "I just...I need more time."

"Darling." He kissed her forehead, then stepped away. "You awakened in me a man that I always wanted to be. I am a better man because of you, Amelia. But just like all the tragedy makes you want to push me away, it makes me want to hold you close. The absurd irony is that these past two years, I've needed you more. And I realize now that you've needed me less."

"I need you, Roark."

For the first time, his eyes filled. "I'm sorry, Ames. I just can't be Seth. I just can't wait for you for years only to have you break my heart."

The door to the house opened. Darek and her father, along with Jace and Max—interesting—came out of the house.

"We're going to Casper's house!" Her father lifted his hand to her. "Roark, come with us."

Roark cocked his head at her. "I wish all the good things for you, darling. Goodbye." Then he turned and walked out of her life.

"You've got to be kidding me."

If Owen hadn't been standing in the foyer with him, well, Casper might have taken a match to the entire place.

"So, usually there is heat in this place?" Owen's words came out in a puff of ice.

"Funny." Casper headed through the front room, spotting the lacy fingers forming on the windows, the chill permeating through his coat as he opened the basement door and headed down the rickety stairs to the furnace.

"Are you sure these are safe to walk on?" Owen said from the top.

"Not even a little," Casper snapped as he flicked on the single bulb in the dirt-walled room.

"This is where the alien appears from behind the hot water heater to rip out your lungs."

"Wow, are you three?"

"Just saying. This place smells like a tomb. Maybe you already buried the aliens."

"Yes. All of them. Sheesh, the house is a hundred years old, Owen, what do you expect?"

Casper found the flashlight he kept under the stairwell and shined it around the room. He'd moved the washing machine and dryer from their former place under a grimy, tiny basement window, but an old soapstone utility tub still stood near the stairs to the storm cellar door. Above it, old cast iron pipes ran to the back of the basement, where the coal-converted-to-gas furnace stood like an old, grumpy soldier.

One whose pilot light had clearly gone out. Maybe even sometime yesterday, when he'd been working on the ceiling. The house had cooled down in the frigid temperatures of the night.

The stairs squeaked as Owen came down them, but Casper was already kneeling before the furnace. "C'mon, old buddy. Don't give out on me."

"Do you think the pipes are frozen?"

"Do you think you could stop voicing my worst nightmare?"

"Maybe I'll just check for aliens." But Owen crouched behind him. "Pilot light is out."

Casper just looked at him. Owen held up his hands. "Trying to help here."

"If you want to help, find me a match. Upstairs, in the kitchen, I think."

"Aye, aye." Owen got up and Casper reached in, flicking the pilot switch off. In a few moments, the gas would dissipate, and he could relight the burner.

He blew out a breath, trying to forget the look on Raina's face as he'd left today. It wasn't like he wanted to leave, but...

"What's going on down here?"

The voice of his father turned him, and Casper had nothing as his father tromped down the stairs, followed by Darek, Jace, Max—huh—and Roark?

"What is this, a party?"

Owen came down the stairs. "Intervention. All I found was this book of matches from the VFW."

His dad gave Casper a thin smile. "We thought you might need a little help."

And with that simple sentence, suddenly the fingers in Casper's chest released. He hadn't even known he'd been sort of holding his breath, or maybe just clenching everything inside him.

Waiting for something else to go wrong.

No, waiting for life to derail, again.

"We saw the fresh drywall upstairs," Darek said. "I thought you were farther than that."

"He was. There was an accident in the upstairs bathroom," Owen said and handed Casper the book of matches.

His father crouched in front of the pilot light mechanism. "Let's check that fuel intake valve. Got any tools?"

"I have an entire Lowe's upstairs."

"Now we're talking." His dad stood and headed toward the stairs.

And Casper was twelve again, helping his father around the house.

He followed him upstairs, along with his brothers.

"What happened?" Darek asked, looking at the ceiling.

"A little plumbing mishap."

"Grace said that Raina said you were almost finished with this place." Max was looking at the ruined floor.

"I was. I am." Casper winced, shook his head. "I have to rebuild the bathroom floor and drywall and paint the ceiling. And relay the flooring and please, God, I'm hoping the pipes haven't burst with the cold—" He ran his hand across his mouth. "I made a stupid promise to my wife and now I'm in over my head."

"Who hasn't made stupid promises to their wife?" Darek said.

"Yeah, but this is different. Raina really needs this. Especially after..." And then, crazily, horrifyingly, his chest tightened. But now everyone was looking at him, and...

"After what, son?"

He looked at his dad and his throat burned. "After we lost the baby."

No one moved. Darek stared at him, hard, and Max frowned. Owen looked away, Jace's mouth made a grim line, and his father drew in a long breath. Roark looked from brother to brother, clearly confused.

"You lost a baby, mate?"

He looked at Roark. Nodded. "It was three months ago. We'd tried for so long before we had Rhett, we didn't think...anyway, Rhett was four months old. But you know Raina—she wants a tribe, so she was thrilled."

"I was at the house, working, and didn't have my phone with me, and she was trying to call me. But I had my power tools going and I didn't hear the phone and by the time I got her calls, it had been a couple hours, and she'd already lost the baby. Miscarried on the bathroom floor."

"I'm sorry, Casp," Darek said. "I had no idea."

"Did she go to the hospital?" Jace asked.

"Yeah. Mom and Dad came over to watch the kids. But ever since, she's been different. She's grieving, but she won't let me in." And he didn't want to let his family into their private life, but, "She doesn't want...we're not..."

He looked away.

More silence.

"The worst part is that there was a lot of damage done when she miscarried and the doctor says she'll probably never be able to carry another child."

"Oh, Casp," Max said.

He shook his head. "It was terrible—seeing all the blood. I was...It was..." He blew out a breath. "I was so glad she was okay, the miscarriage didn't hit me like it did Raina. That, or of course, the fact that we won't have any more kids."

There. It was out. But it still didn't shut down the terrible roaring that suddenly tunneled through him.

No more kids.

"I'm sorry," his dad said. "We knew about the miscarriage, but we felt that it was your news to tell. And of course, we didn't know about...well, the rest."

"It's fine."

"No, it's not." And then, like he might be twelve, his father walked over and simply embraced him.

Just put his arms around him, like he might be a child.

Shoot, he just stood there. He needed this, and that realization shook him. Needed someone to just hold him up for a minute.

Finally, he pushed away, looked at his dad. "I'm okay."

"I know." He gave him a grim nod.

"I just...I don't know how to fix this. I thought maybe

moving from our little house in town to this...this place might..." He looked at the ceiling. "It's a money pit. And I spend every waking moment here, outside of work, and she told me today she hates this house, and I might hate it too." He walked over to his toolbox, on the floor, and pulled out a pair of pliers. "Fact is, I think I'm making everything worse." He handed the pliers to his dad. "I don't know how you did it, Dad. Because I'm not good at...I guess being a husband. A dad. All of it."

"Take a breath, son."

"No, he's right," Max said. He went over and sat on the edge of the windowsill. "Grace wants me to enroll in this experimental procedure for Huntington's, but it's risky, and it could go south, and all I can think of is abandoning her and Yulia— but if I don't do it, I'm giving up—"

"You're not giving up. You're doing what's best for your family," Darek said. "Sometimes you have to make the unpopular decision, or at least the hard decision to keep everyone safe."

"But it's not about you," Owen said quietly. He looked at Darek, then Casper and finally Max. "It's about the promise you made to your wife. What she needs."

"What if she doesn't let you do what she needs," Roark said. "What if she just pushes you away and..." He shook his head. "I shouldn't be talking. I don't have a wife."

"You support her. You keep trying," Jace said. "It's like when you're on the ice—you have to block for her, keep her out of trouble."

"Oh, I think it's Scotty who keeps me out of trouble," Owen said.

Casper smiled, and Owen's words elicited a few chuckles.

"But sometimes, I dunno, I think maybe I cause the trouble too." Jace made a face. "Eden is pregnant. And the doctor says the baby not only has Down syndrome but has a major heart defect."

Silence, and Casper had never seen Jace look so, suddenly, defeated. Owen looked at him with something of horror. Max shook his head.

"Wow," Darek said.

"Sorry," Casper said.

"She told me not to tell anyone, so I'm asking you all to go down with the ship with me." Jace made a face. "I used to think we could handle anything, but this one has thrown Eden, and I feel like I keep making everything worse. I don't know how to, well…" He met Casper's gaze. "Fix it, I guess."

"Boys," John said quietly. "You're overthinking this. No one asked you to fix everything, or know all the answers, or always meet all your wife's needs. Life is full of suffering and hard decisions, and…sure, you can try— You can listen and protect and sacrifice and show up, but the fact is, the reason you ask God into your marriage is because *you will fail.* You're not your wife's savior. God is. It's up to Him to fix it."

"Joseph," Darek said.

Casper looked at him. "Joseph?"

"As in Mary and Joseph? Talk about being in over your head, right? He finds out the woman he loves is pregnant—not his kid —but he still marries her."

Casper managed not to look at Owen.

"After a dream," Max said. "Telling him it was the right thing to do."

"And then he has another dream, telling him to run to Egypt —" Roark said.

"Are you saying we need to sleep more?" Owen said, grinning.

Darek gave him a look.

"The point," his dad said, "is that God directed Joseph when he needed it. And He'll do the same for you. Jesus is the Messiah, and while the end goal of Christmas is salvation, He is also Emmanuel—God with us. Now, today, every step of this journey. None of us are alone." He looked at Casper, then Darek, Owen, Jace, Roark, and finally at Max.

Max met his gaze, something in it that Casper couldn't read.

His dad walked over to Max. Put his hand on his shoulder. "You're entering a battle, Max. And maybe we all needed a moment to stop and realize that, because we are with you in this battle. I can promise you that you—and Grace and Yulia—will not be abandoned. Not by us, and not by God."

Max swallowed, looked away, nodding.

"All right, then. I'm going to go clean out the fuel injector on the furnace. And then I'm going to call Ingrid and tell her not to expect us for dinner. Casper has a promise to keep."

Casper watched his father leave the room. What—?

"Yeah, he does," Owen said, holding up his fist.

Darek bumped it. "Supplies are in the kitchen. Roark, do you know how to tile?"

"He really said that?" Eden said. She sat cross-legged on the old, braided carpet in the basement, gluing a tiny fabric curtain to a Popsicle stick, the hot glue beading up on the wooden surface.

She'd already glued her thumb and finger together, twice, but she was getting it. Across from her, Ivy was cutting rickrack for the roofline, and Scotty was peeling some ready-to-glue wallpaper. Grace had left after dinner with Yulia, about the same time Raina did.

Poor Amelia. Eden didn't know what to make of the tangled explanation she gave of her argument with Roark.

Who'd left.

Left?

"Yes. He said he couldn't be Seth." Amelia leaned against the old green sofa, her feet drawn up, her arms around her knees. At least she'd stopped sobbing.

"I can't believe he left you standing there in the yard," Ivy said. "I remember when he showed up the first time—he practically barged into the house. Are you sure he compared himself to Seth?"

"Who is Seth?" Scotty said.

When her mother had uncovered her current art project—the reconstruction of the old Barbie dollhouse the girls had used for years, repainting it and redecorating with new carpet remnants, curtains, and furniture—Scotty had dived in with a DIY vigor.

Eden had no doubt it was one of her mother's 'distract and chat' techniques—she well remembered being dragged into some kind of project every time she needed to unload a problem.

"Seth was her boyfriend from high school," her mother said. "He just married Ree a couple weeks ago." She looked at Amelia. "Of course Roark isn't Seth. You chose Roark, and Seth ended up with the right girl."

"So what did he mean, by saying he couldn't be Seth?" Scotty said. She'd finished gluing a new sheet of rose-printed wallpaper on the little girls' room, and now smoothed it down. Hard to believe that usually she skippered a ship on brutal, frigid seas.

"I don't know!"

Eden did. "Honey. You dated Seth because he was safe. And fun and cute, but really, he was safe. He was your hometown."

"Seth had our lives all planned out...here. But I was called to something bigger."

"Yes. But you never truly settled your heart on Seth, and..." Eden lifted a shoulder. "And then Roark walked into your life and you knew you wanted someone—a life—that was larger."

"I wanted to do something that mattered. And I felt God calling me to that life. *With* Roark."

"Seven years, Amelia," Ivy said. "I hate to be the lawyer here, but...seven years."

Amelia stared at her, her mouth in a tight line. "You haven't seen what I've seen."

Ivy set down the scissors. "No. I haven't. I've seen a lot, but not... I know you've seen some terrible things. And my guess is that you might even have a little PTSD. But you know who has seen what you've seen? Roark. He clearly loves you and still wants a life with you. I know that I couldn't imagine going through any of that without the person I loved."

"I love him!" She drew in a breath, schooled her voice. "I do love him..."

"But?" her mother said.

"But..." She looked at her mother, then Eden. "I...I'm...I don't want..." She shrugged. "I just like the way things are— were—between us. Working side by side, partners at Hope Children's Village and all the other orphanages and schools of Compassion Constantine."

"And that will change if you get married?" her mother said.

Amelia swallowed. "I am the one called to missions. He followed me, remember? And, Roark watched his parents die in a brutal attack." She raised her gaze to her mother, then the others. "We've spent the past six years in war-torn countries, watching families split apart, children dying. The truth is— sorry, Mom—that we live in dangerous areas. What if he decides that..." She sighed. "What if we have kids and Roark decides that life is over? That it's too dangerous."

"I think I'm getting this. You get married...you have a child... and your life as missionaries is over," Ivy said quietly. "Wow, that was some hard math, there, Ames."

"I've had a hard time admitting that to myself too," Amelia said. "My career over family? It sounds so selfish. But what we do is important..."

"It's not terrible to not want to give up the life you have," Scotty said quietly.

"Or to want to follow the career you worked so hard on," Ivy added, just as quietly.

"Consider this," their mom said. "God knows your heart. He called you to missions. And that desire is still in your heart. If God wants you to do something different, He'll change your desires."

"Will He? Because Seth was single a long time after I left him."

"He just got married to a woman he wildly loves," Ivy said.

Her mother nodded. "God can change your desires...if you are willing to give them to Him."

"You might consider telling Roark your feelings," Scotty said quietly.

"That I don't want to marry him because I think he'll wreck my life? Yes, that will go over well."

"Amelia, honey. Stop making decisions about a future that may never happen." Upstairs, the phone rang. Her mother headed up the stairs.

"Roark came all the way across the ocean to tell you that it's over. Honey, it's not remotely over," Eden said.

"You think so?" Amelia asked.

"Please," Scotty said. "I don't even know the guy, and I could see how much pain he was in. He would rather lose a limb than walk away from you."

"Maybe he's still in town," Amelia said. "He left with the guys when they went over to Casper's house."

"Oh, my bet is that they corralled him into some sort of project," Ivy said.

Eden glanced at Ivy. "Have you really been appointed to be a judge?"

Ivy finished cutting the rickrack. "Yes. But I don't think I'll be accepting."

"What? Why not?" Eden set down the curtain and grabbed another Popsicle stick.

"Because of your dad. I mean, it's just...it's not right for us to leave. Not if he doesn't have help." She said it without accusation, not even a glance at Scotty.

"What do you mean? My dad is pretty capable." But she wasn't. Shoot, she burned her finger again. She put down the glue gun, put her finger in her mouth.

"Yeah, but maybe not for much longer. Darek says he doesn't know how sick he is, so..." Ivy lifted a shoulder. "I just don't think we can leave him."

But Eden's heart had stopped on *how sick he is*. "My dad is sick?"

Scotty unpeeled another piece of wallpaper. "Yeah, that's why we came home. Because Amelia called Owen."

Eden looked at her sister. "You called Owen and not me?"

Amelia's mouth opened. "I figured you knew. You came home early, and you and mom are so close..."

"Apparently not that close. How sick *is* Dad? What kind of sick?" Eden looked at Ivy. "Mom said they went to the Mayo Clinic in October, but she said everything was great."

"Yeah, well, you know your dad. Darek thinks if it was something serious, he wouldn't tell us until he'd figured out everything."

"I heard them talking about not wanting to tell us until after Christmas," Amelia said. And Mom said it might be too late— that he might already be gone."

Eden just blinked at her. Then, "Okay, we need to talk to Mom."

"Owen said that we should wait until after Christmas—"

"I don't care what Owen said!" Eden said and got up.

And then, she stilled.

She didn't need to see her sisters' expressions to know something was wrong—very wrong—because she could feel the heat, the wetness on her leg.

"Eden," Ivy said. "You're bleeding."

8

A fire crackled in the giant stone hearth of Grace's home, the scent of gingerbread cookies spiced the great room, and Michael Bublé sang "Cold December Night" from Max's impressive stereo system.

They'd put up a real tree right after Thanksgiving, and tonight Grace had watered it, refreshing the fragrance of pine in the house. It glittered against the timber walls of the home and rose two stories to nearly touch the beams that spanned the vaulted ceiling.

It was all systems go at the Sharpe house, but as Grace stood in front of her double oven, watching the cookies bake, she couldn't feel it. Not with Max still gone, and the wind starting to howl against the massive windows that overlooked beautiful Deep Haven.

Yulia had vanished to her room, probably to watch a movie on her tablet, and maybe Grace should get her, see if she wanted to watch *A Christmas Story*, one of Max's favorites, but really, they should watch it with Max.

This is how it was going to be. Her longing for Max, the

terrible ache inside only growing larger as each day he lost more of his life.

Grace pulled the final tray of cookies from the oven and set it on a hot pad on her massive island.

Max had built her a gourmet kitchen worthy of a Michelin star chef, but she'd barely used it lately.

Until today.

"Wow, Mom, seriously?"

Grace looked up to see Yulia come down the stairs. Their great room opened two stories to a massive stairway that led up to two equally massive bedrooms with en suites—one for Max and Grace, the other for Yulia.

Max had also wanted a bedroom on the main floor, which he currently used as his office, for when he couldn't use the stairs.

He'd also installed an elevator down to the lower floor, which held the theater, a workout room, a sauna, another office, and what he called the hammock porch, where everyone had their own lounger that overlooked the patio, with the in-ground hot tub.

She'd never imagined living in such a beautiful home, but then again, she'd never imagined her life with a man like Max.

Who, up until this week, lived life full throttle, face to the wind, tasting everything he could.

Yulia walked over to the island. "I count four different kinds of cookies. And enough gingerbread men to launch an assault on Deep Haven." She picked one up and slid onto a stool. She'd pulled on a wool hat, her tawny brown hair shiny and long. Oh, she was growing into a beauty—please let Max be here long enough to watch her fall in love, get married.

Be a grandfather.

The thought pressed a dagger into her heart. See, it was better not to think.

"I was..." But she didn't have an answer as she slid the last gingerbread man onto the cooling rack.

"Worried." Yulia bit off one of the heads. "Dad will be fine. He fell, but you heard the doctor. It was just an accident."

"I know. And he's with your uncles. It's just...the house feels so big. And it sounds like there might be a blizzard on the way." She nearly shivered, despite the heat in the house. Outside, the wind whistled.

No, the chill came from within, from the hollow space where hope used to live. *Show me the story, Lord.*

Yulia slid off the stool. "The ski hill is making snow, and a bunch of friends are going skiing tomorrow. I want to go."

Grace looked at her. "What? No—"

"I'm on holiday break, Mom. And there's nothing to do around here."

"Your dad will be home!"

Yulia frowned. "He's home every day."

"He's been in the hospital for two days."

"Because you made him. Because you freaked out about him dying already and made him stay there and..." She finished her cookie. "Mom. He's not dead yet. And I want to go skiing."

"It's Christmas."

"Christmas is technically six days away. I promise to be back by then."

She didn't know what possessed her. Maybe it was the way Yulia was standing there—looking so composed, so *not* undone by her father's illness, so, well, full of life, and yes, a little sassy—that something inside Grace simply snapped.

"Fine!" And suddenly, in a move she didn't recognize, she pushed the tray of cookies off the counter and onto the floor. "Go. Be with your friends. Clearly, they're more important than your parents. Or whoever we are."

Yulia's eyes widened. She slid off the chair, breathing hard, turned, and took off up the stairs.

Grace closed her eyes, then put her hands over her face. Her knees buckled and she sank onto the floor and sobbed.

She knew what she'd signed up for. Had agreed to it. But...

"Oh, Grace, what happened?"

She looked up to see Max crouched in front of her. He'd shucked off his jacket and boots, but still wore his hat, so maybe he'd heard the last of the fight.

Oh, he was handsome, with that dark hair curling out the back of his hat, those brown eyes that turned to shades of caramel in the morning sun. Two days in the hospital had left a dark grizzle on his chin, and he wore a black thermal shirt, from the change of clothes she'd brought him today, and a pair of worn jeans. He smelled faintly of wood chips and hard work.

He simply sat down and pulled her over to him, right there on the kitchen floor, wrapping his arms around her. Despite his fall, he hadn't lost any muscle it seemed, every inch of him toned, solid, an athlete.

Oh, it wasn't fair, this terrible disease.

"Babe. Why are the gingerbread men all over the floor? Are they making a break for it?"

She wanted to laugh, but it only made her cry harder.

"Okay, okay." He kissed her head. "I know it's been a long week."

She settled against him. He smelled good—perfect, really. But—

"Is this drywall dust on your shirt?" She wiped away a smattering of white on his sleeve, stretched nicely over his bicep.

He flexed for her, and oh, she couldn't help it and laughed between her sobs. What a wreck.

"Casper is in a bit of a mess at the house. We pitched in and helped him get it back in shape."

"You too?"

"Yeah. Of course." He lifted her chin and found her eyes. "I know you think that I'm falling apart, but I'm far from incapable, Grace. I promise." He smiled and his gaze fell to her lips.

Bent—

Oh, she didn't know why she stopped him, but she found her hand on his chest and her eyes back on his. "Max, I…I'm just so scared. Aren't you?"

He sighed. "I'm only scared that somehow I won't hang on tight enough to God. We're not the only family who is going to go through hard times—life is about suffering. And frankly, we've been given the opportunity to prepare for it. Think of everyone out there who is blindsided by it."

Like Darek, when Felicity died. Or Owen, when he'd lost his eye. And even Roark, when his entire family had been killed. So, "But…now that you're not doing the treatment, all I see ahead is…it's just dark."

"Babe. Your dad reminded me tonight that it's only dark because we imagine going through suffering alone. We are afraid because we know we'll crumple. And we might. But that's when God catches us. Provides. Guides. This journey, even in suffering, can bring us joy when we end up in the arms of our Father. Which is where we *will* end up. Right?"

She sort of wanted to end up right here, in Max's arms. But, "Yes."

"Babe. This is just the *start* of our forever. Fear not… For unto us, is born this day…a Savior."

Right. "Tidings of great joy."

"Great. *Joy.*" His gaze held hers. "I used to think God gave me a throwaway life. But this life with you, Gracie, is a life worth fighting for."

And then he kissed her again.

This time, she let him, and the kiss was all Max: bright, bold, full of life, not giving up, not giving in, and especially a man who could make her feel as if the world was perfect and golden and, well, Christmas.

He lingered, finding places on her neck, behind her ear, under her eye. "You smell really good. Like cinnamon and nutmeg…" He met her eyes. Winked.

She grinned. Oh Max. "Yes. But first I need to talk to our daughter. Yulia wants to go skiing tomorrow and..." She made a face.

He glanced at the debris on the floor. "Innocents were caught in the crossfire."

"Something like that."

"I'll give them a decent burial. You fix things with our daughter." He kissed her again. "I don't hate the idea of a day home alone with you."

She headed up the stairs, humming Bublé. *So kiss me on this cold December night...*

On the island her phone vibrated. She was at the top of the stairs when Max called out. "Hon? You'd better hurry. Your mom just texted."

She looked down, over the railing, to where he was eating one of her non-sacrificed soldiers. "What?"

"She says that Eden is in the ER."

She stood, staring at him. "Why would Eden be in the ER?"

He lifted a shoulder. "I dunno. Maybe it has something to do with her pregnancy?"

"Eden is pregnant?" She came back down the stairs. "How do you know this?"

"Can't tell you. I would betray the oath of brotherhood—"

"Max—"

"Jace. Jace told me. And apparently the baby has some complications."

Grace swiped up the car keys, but Max grabbed her arm, pulled her close. "There were flurries in the air when Owen drove me home. Please be careful. I think we're heading into a blizzard."

She kissed him, lingered, then pulled away. "Then keep the fire going for me."

"Always." He winked and she smiled as she went back out into the cold.

❄

This wasn't quite what Darek had in mind when he'd wished for snow. Prayed for it? He couldn't remember. Although it added a needed ambiance to the resort, especially this close to Christmas. They had a handful of guests staying the week, but the resort was unusually slow for the holiday season.

A little snow might boost sales.

But an all-out blizzard could turn deadly. And, as Darek walked out of Casper's house to go home, a frigid wind caught him, burning his nose. He pulled up the collar of his jacket and hunched over against it as Roark followed him out and down the steps. Already, snow had started to accumulate.

"Aw, crumb," Roark said. "I should have started back earlier. I got pulled in by all this chumminess."

"Back where?" Darek asked as he pulled out an ice scraper from behind his front seat. He handed it to Roark, who was trying to scrape off the snow from his rental car with a credit card.

"I have a hotel in Duluth tonight. Couldn't find a place in Deep Haven."

Darek stilled. "Duluth? What—no, you can stay with Ivy and me. It's too far to drive back and forth every day. It's three hours—"

"I'm not coming back." Roark walked over to the other side of the car.

"You're not...?" Darek frowned. Okay, maybe Ivy had been right when she'd said something wasn't quite right today. He'd been known to miss the details—like his dad's illness. Although he'd seemed just fine tonight when he'd cleaned out Casper's igniter and got the pilot light fired up again. By tomorrow, the house would be warm enough for the paint to dry.

And Casper would be keeping promises to his wife. Hooyah! That's how the Christiansen boys got it done.

Including Roark, who *had* tiled before and helped him tile and grout the new floor of Casper's bathroom.

Roark continued to clear the snow off the car, now the hood, as he came around. "Amelia and I broke up."

Maybe he didn't hear him right. Darek just stood there. "You...what?"

Roark handed him back the scraper. "We broke up."

"Roark. Wait...you can't break up. You've been together six years. You're engaged—"

"Yeah, mate. For *six* years. I dunno what that looks like to you, but to me that says she might love me but she doesn't want to marry me."

"Dude. She wants to marry you."

Roark raised an eyebrow. "I've been trying to get her to set a date for two years. I don't care when. It could be tomorrow night. Next week. Valentine's Day—something to know that there will be a day when she is my wife."

Darek raised an eyebrow even as he took back the scraper. "I'm going to give you the benefit of the doubt here, but that sounds a little—"

"Desperate? Demanding. Yes. As you'd say, you betcha. I know this might be a hard concept for you, Darek, but we're *waiting*. Have been waiting for seven years."

"Watch yourself, there, mate."

"I'm just saying that after a while, a guy starts to wonder how long he has to wait."

Sometimes Darek had to remind himself that Roark was about his age, and yes, maybe a guy in his early thirties might like to be married and start a family. Still, "Until she says yes. My sister *is* only twenty-six. And you knew that when you chased her across an ocean."

"Yes," Roark said, sighing. "I do know that. And I've waited. And I would still wait for her if I thought that someday she'd say yes. But I...maybe I've had my eyes opened. Amelia loves me—

I'm sure of that. She just doesn't love me enough to marry me. Just like her old boyfriend, Seth."

Darek's eyes widened. "Wait—Seth?"

"Yes. She led him on too—"

"She did not lead Seth on."

"He was waiting for her, here, for years—"

"Hey, I like Seth, but I knew he wasn't right for her. She didn't lead him on...she was just too afraid to break his heart."

Roark met his gaze.

Oh.

"Don't do this. Amelia is an amazing woman—"

"That she is. And I have no doubt she will follow God with all her heart. Just not with me." He looked away, closed his eyes. Drew in a breath.

"Roark—"

He held out his hand. "All the best to you, Darek, and your family." Roark's mouth was a tight, grim line.

Darek's throat burned. But he took his hand. "It's late. Why don't you stay tonight with us?"

"I have an early flight back to London tomorrow," he said. "My uncle Donovan is expecting me for the holidays." He opened his door. "And I guess I need to ask God what He wants from me now."

Darek had a husband's answer for him. But Roark wasn't a husband, despite his commitment to Amelia. So he stepped back and lifted his hand as Roark backed away, down the driveway...

And into the night.

He should have said something, done something...

The thought tunneled into him the entire drive home, back to his cute bungalow in Deep Haven where his beautiful wife, the one he didn't deserve, had left the light on for him. The snowman in the front yard had taken a hard fall into a snowdrift, now covered in a layer of snow and ice. He knew the feeling.

Inside, however, he found his dinner of chili in the refrigerator.

It was unfathomable to him that Amelia and Roark wouldn't end up together. But also that Jace and Eden had a child who might not live past the womb, or Casper and Raina and their loss, that they hadn't shared with anyone, and of course, Max and Grace and the inescapable struggle before them.

Darek closed the fridge, not hungry.

Wow, he wished he could figure out a way to fix...something.

Funny, Ivy hadn't come out to greet him, so he headed down the hall to where the light barely shone out under their door. Joy's room was open, so he looked in, and was then drawn to her bed where she lay, asleep. He pulled up another blanket over her as the blizzard rattled her panes. Old windows. He'd promised Ivy new windows, but of course, they wouldn't need those now.

Tiger's light was on, and he knocked, and then opened the door. Tiger sat with headphones on, watching his phone. He pulled one earbud out. "Hey, Dad. A bunch of the kids are going skiing tomorrow. Can I go?"

"What did your mom say?"

"Yes."

"Then, yes."

Tiger raised a fist as Darek shut the door.

The very fact that Tiger had a mom to ask *tharrumped* through him.

Would he have waited six years for Ivy? Maybe.

But he was a much less patient man than Roark, and he had Tiger to show for that, so maybe not.

Yeah, good thing fixing everything wasn't up to him, but... wow, he couldn't help but try.

He opened his door, expecting his wife to be sitting up in bed watching television or maybe scrolling on her phone.

Instead, she was sitting up in bed, her knees drawn up, clutching a pillow.

"Ivy?"

The bedside light cast over her, her reddened cheeks, the tears—

"What's wrong?" He sat on the bed. "Honey."

She leaned into him as his arms closed around her. "I'm turning it down."

"What—?" He pushed her away. "Please don't tell me you're turning down the judgeship."

She nodded and he held his hands up, got up from the bed. "Stop. No. We had a deal—"

"That was before you told me that your dad is dying."

He blinked at her. And now she was out of bed, dressed in her flannel pajamas, her red hair wild around her head, a little fire in her green eyes.

Oh, this wasn't sad crying. It was mad crying.

And he was the target.

"Ivy—"

"For Pete's sake I'm a Christiansen too, and, and—I'm not going to let you sell the resort. Because that's what's going to happen, isn't it?"

He sighed. "Probably."

"No." She shook her head. "No—"

"Yes!" He didn't mean to raise his voice, but—"Your life, your needs are important to me—"

"More important than this legacy, your family—?"

"Yes."

She stared at him, then sank onto the bed. "I don't..." Then she closed her eyes, her hands over them. "Oh, Darek, I can't be the bad guy here. I can't be the one who puts an end to your family's heritage."

He found himself on his knees in front of her. "You're not. It's just...how life is turning out."

"I could commute."

"That's not a life for us. Our marriage. Our kids—"

"Exactly. So, there's only one answer."

"We sell the resort—"

"I turn down the appointment—"

"No, Ivy. *No.*" He took her hands. "Listen. Ten years from now, I'll still be chopping wood, praying for snow, trying to keep guests happy, where you might be...I don't know, a federal judge. You could end up on the Supreme Court!"

"I highly doubt that—"

"I don't. And the last thing I want is for you to regret..." He swallowed, looked away. "I held it against my first wife that she made me quit being a hot shot. I resented her for it and..."

"I know you regret that, Dare. But this isn't that. I won't resent you—"

"You don't know that."

"Yes, I do. I love my life. This life—with you, with these children. Remember—before I met you, I had no one. You gave me...everything." Tears dripped down her face.

"I think God gave us everything." He held her face, thumbing a tear off it. "But it doesn't mean that there isn't more waiting for us, even if we have to let this go."

She blinked at him.

He pulled her close, molding her flannelled body to his. "I know God will fix this. I believe it."

Then he took her face in his hands again and kissed her. She was salty and tender and yielding, and who needed chili when he had a warm, sweet wife waiting for him?

"I love you, Darek Christiansen."

"See? I'm so worth the price."

She laughed and tugged on his shirt, pulling him back with her onto their thick, warm comforter.

He caught himself on his hands, staring down at his beautiful wife with her red hair splayed over the white flannel comforter, at the twinkle in her eyes, at her smile and…and…

He rolled away. "I keep thinking about Roark and the fact that he and Amelia broke up."

"I know." She sat up next to him. "She told us."

He touched her hand on his chest. "How is she doing?"

"I think she's going to try to talk to him."

"He left for Duluth."

She sat back, frowned. "She went looking for him in town."

"It's pretty slick out there. I invited him to stay here, but he was set on leaving."

She tucked her finger into Darek's collar. "Well, I'm glad you made it home. How'd it go at Casper's house?"

He followed her nudge and rolled back over, propping one hand up, the other tucked under her head. "Fine." He kissed her neck, her cheek, her lips. Okay, now he was focused.

He couldn't fix his family. But he could fix this. He smiled at her.

She smiled back and wrapped her arms around his neck. "C'mere."

The wind howled outside, but the house was safe and warm and—

"Is that your phone?" she said into his ear.

He lifted his head and reached into his back pocket. Pulled it out. Sat up.

"Oh no."

She sat up, even as he climbed out of their warm bed. "It's Pete Dahlquist. He's calling out the CRT and fire team. There's been a bad accident just outside of town."

He'd left her.

Roark had actually, truly left her.

Amelia had driven into town in the resort truck, her windshield wipers on high as the blizzard—it was really starting to blow—softened the curves and slicked the highway into town.

She'd nearly hit a Caravan on its way out of town that slid through the stoplight at Main Street. She couldn't help but think of the tragedy over a year ago that had taken out the fish house.

A year ago, when she'd been home with Roark to set a date and look at wedding venues. Instead, she'd dodged any commitment, anxious to start work at their new school in Nigeria.

And Roark hadn't pushed.

In fact, he'd never pushed. He'd waited. He'd listened. He'd protected and...

Oh, she was such a fool.

Because the character of Roark was to wait. To listen. To protect...and to care about her feelings.

What did she think—that he'd change once they got married? And, her mother was right...God *could* change her desires. And if not, He could even protect her in a foreign land.

Because, well, *Mary.*

She swiped at the moisture in her eyes as she pulled out of the East Harbor Hotel parking lot. It was full, but none of the cars had the green Florida plates of Roark's rental Jeep. She remembered clearly because she couldn't get past the thought of...what was a Florida car doing here—even as Roark drove out of her life.

Because, maybe, she hadn't believed it.

Now, as she eased down the road to the final hotel—the Best Western—his words hung in her heart, like the resonance of a gong. *I wish all the good things for you, darling. Goodbye.*

Roark. I'm sorry!

She should probably be at the hospital, but what was she

going to do to help Eden? Her mother had taken her in, although the bleeding had sort of stopped, so it might be nothing.

Except, high risk baby, and poor Eden. Talk about giving up her career—she had a second novel coming out.

And, c'mon, Amelia, that wasn't the important part.

Please, God, protect Eden's baby!

She crept through the Best Western parking lot, saw a car from Missouri, but the rest of the plates were either Wisconsin or Minnesota so...

Roark was gone.

She sat, the car humming, the rhythm of the windshield wipers pushing back the snow that whistled down the street. It had accumulated in drifts, small, but by morning they'd be tiny waves flowing through town.

The entire population of Deep Haven would be socked in, hopefully nestled under blankets, sitting in front of a fire, in their warm houses—

We're going to Casper's house! Roark, come with us.

He wouldn't have...really?

Maybe. She turned up the street, out of town. Almost a whiteout now, but she knew the road. Still, she braked long in advance when she spotted red lights ahead. Red, flashing lights.

An accident on the highway. Which meant cars piled up and if Roark was still at the house, he'd be long gone before she got there.

She turned off, crawled through the streets and finally came out at another road, this one north of town.

The back road was nearly drifted over, but she had the truck, and eased along the road. No other tire tracks evidenced any getaways, but when she pulled up to Casper's house, only his truck remained in the drive.

But the light was on.

She got out and ducked her head down into her scarf, then slipped up the walk, nearly falling, but grabbed the railing in time and skated up the stairs.

"Casper!" Opening the door, she stuck her head inside. "Hello the house!"

No answer.

She went inside and stamped off her boots. The place looked nearly finished. A massive patch of wall and ceiling had been freshly drywalled, mudded, and sanded, and the ceiling had been painted, given the drop cloths on the floor. "Casper?"

"Up here!"

She followed the voice up the staircase. Wow, she'd heard Casper talk about this place, with its winding staircase, and beautiful oak floor and ornate trim, the sense of grandeur, but really, this was a real work of art.

He was on his hands and knees, sponging off grout in the bathroom.

"Nice bathroom, Casp."

"Thanks." He sat back and squeezed out his sponge into a bucket. "I had a plumbing catastrophe a couple days ago, but I think we're almost back in shape." He looked tired, his hair whitened with dust, more than three days of whiskers on his chin. But he smiled at her, and something had definitely changed since the last time she saw him earlier that day.

"Raina will love it."

"I hope so." He started wiping again. "Your boy Roark did all the grout work. He's a keeper."

And just like that, her eyes filled. She pressed her hand to her mouth. Nodded.

He glanced up at her, frowned. "Ames?"

She shook her head.

He put the sponge down and stood up. "What's going on?" And then he pulled her to himself.

Aw. She and Casper hadn't been close—he'd always been sort of the mysterious one, off on his escapades as a treasure hunter. But he was the brother who had most closely shared her desire to leave Deep Haven and...well, do something. Missions for her, treasures for him, although put together in one thought, it didn't sound that different. Searching for lost souls, lost treasures.

"Roark broke up with me."

Casper said nothing, just kept his arms around her.

"Did you hear me?"

"I heard your words, but...that doesn't make sense. Roark was here. All night. He left with Darek about a half hour ago."

Darek? "Do you think he's staying with him?"

"I don't know. Why?"

"It's really blizzardy out."

"It is?" Casper let her go and walked over to the window. "Wow. There's snow out there."

"A lot of snow. And it's really coming down. There's an accident on the highway out of town."

Casper frowned at her, then headed down the stairs.

"Where are you going?"

"I'm a volunteer firefighter. And on the Crisis Response Team. If they needed help, they would have texted." He walked through to the kitchen, and she followed him inside.

"Wow. This is as nice as Grace's kitchen." She ran her hand over a massive quartz island. A six-burner range sat under a copper hood, and the cabinets ran all the way to the ceiling, nine feet high. "This island holds...what, ten?"

"We wanted a big family."

He was scrolling through his messages. "Why did he break up with you?"

She sighed. "Because I wouldn't marry him."

He looked over at her. "What? You said yes to the engagement—"

"But I kept putting it off and...I don't blame him, really. It's my fault. He's been a champ for six years. I didn't even realize I was leading him on, but..."

"That is a long time. And yes, he is a champ to chase you around the world for that long without an I Do. Shoot. I did get a text. About fifteen minutes ago." Pressing dial, he put the phone to his ear. Looked at her. "So what's holding you back now?"

She drew in a breath. "Nothing. My own stupid fear. I always intended on marrying him, but in the back of my mind, I was afraid that if I married him, somehow I'd lose myself and my calling. But if God knew my heart then, and gave me Roark, I guess I can trust Him with my future."

"Atta girl. Hey. Sorry. I just got the text. You guys still need me?"

She wandered over to the Sub-Zero fridge. Two doors, and a third for a freezer. And then more counter space and more cabinets and a huge pantry.

Apparently, Casper was hoping for a football team.

"Okay. Yes," Casper was saying.

He turned away from her. "Okay, yep, we're on our way."

She pressed her hand on the chill of the island.

Casper turned back. Met her eyes. "We need to go. Right now."

"What? Where?"

"To the hospital."

She nodded, following him out of the room as he swept up his parka, his hat. "Is it Eden?"

He turned, shook his head. "Why Eden?"

"Because she might be having a miscarriage."

He just blinked at her. Then, "Oh no. Okay, well, no. It's not Eden." He walked over, took her hand. Met her eyes. "That was my buddy, Cole. He's with the Deep Haven Crisis Response Team. There was a crash on the highway." He swallowed, looked out the window, back to her.

"It's Grace. She's—"

"No!"

He gripped her shoulders. "Not dead. But hurt. We gotta go."

9

First time Owen met hockey great Jace Jacobsen, enforcer for the Minnesota Blue Ox, he'd been a punk, cocky seventeen-year-old, fresh out of the juniors, trying out for the farm team.

He'd gotten on the ice, talked a little trash to the 6'4" defenseman, as if he weren't scared out of his skin, then tried to juke him out with a slick hockey move.

Jace had put him on his back, right at the blue line, the pipes of the ceiling spinning. Truth was, Jace "J-Hammer" Jacobsen was the toughest guy he knew.

So when Owen returned to Casper's after bringing Max home, and Jace got in the car and picked up his phone from where he'd left it on the dash, when he saw the messages from Eden and asked in a low, shaky tone if they could drive him to the hospital, and then closed his eyes, his hand over his mouth, as if trying to hold it together—yeah, it freaked Owen out. Right to his core.

This. Watching Jace's jaw tighten against the thousands of thoughts rippling through his brain, watching him stare out the window as Owen's father negotiated the slick back roads that wound toward Deep Haven...then watching as Jace texted again, and again, and then again and then tightened his hand around his phone, turning his grip white—this was why Owen and Scotty wouldn't have kids.

It wasn't about Scotty not wanting to be a mom—although that was part of it. And it wasn't about their lifestyle as fishermen—although for sure parenthood and fishing seemed mutually exclusive. It was the fact that Owen well remembered his childhood and his mistakes and had no doubt he'd caused exactly that look on his father's face too many times.

He didn't know how his parents bore it. The endless hockey matches, and later, watching him face off with players who wanted to bloody him. Or even later, when he'd lost his eye, how they stood by as he unraveled his life, destroying others along the way.

No. He and Scotty had enough trouble trying to keep themselves alive, thank you, and this was his thought as his father pulled up to the Deep Haven hospital, the light from the ER gleaming out through the bulleting snow.

Jace was out of the car almost before his father stopped, running and slipping along the sidewalk to the entrance.

They parked and went in, and by then, Jace was in the ER, behind the curtain, dealing with whatever tragedy was happening, so they headed to the lobby.

His mother appeared a moment later, her blonde hair sticking out of a beanie hat, carrying her jacket. She still wore a Christmas sweater, and the little bells on the fringes jangled every time she moved.

She walked right into her husband's embrace. Owen took her jacket, silently, from her, and tossed it into a nearby chair.

"How bad is it?" his father asked. "Jace looked pretty upset."

"You know about the baby?" she asked.

He nodded. "And the birth defects."

"Yes. Well." And that's when she looked at Owen. She gave

him a wan smile. "Your wife is with the kids at the house. She is so amazing with them."

She was?

"I'm so glad you two came for Christmas, Owen. It's so good you're here."

He didn't know why her words reached in and warmed him, filling a space he hadn't known was vacant.

"The bleeding stopped, so they think it might have been just a clot that was lost, but they're doing an ultrasound." She sighed. "Even if she hasn't lost it, it's likely she'll be on bed rest until the baby comes. I think..." She made a face. "I think she'll need me, honey."

His father nodded. Then, strangely, put his forehead to meet hers. "We'll do what we have to. I'm not sure if I can...if I can be there. I'll do my best, though."

Owen looked at them, frowned. What—? Okay, that was enough. "Dad, what do you mean—"

"John!"

The voice cut through his, and Owen turned to see his old friend Kyle Hueston coming through the ER doors.

Kyle glanced over to Owen, and something clicked in his eyes, a blink, a recognition, and then Kyle headed over to John and Ingrid.

"There's been an accident on the highway. The CRT team is there, but the roads are getting pretty slick—I think we need a plow out there, ASAP."

His father glanced at his mother, then turned to Kyle. "Sure. Just—"

"Dad!"

An ambulance had backed up to the door, and Owen stilled, seeing Darek walking in, holding one side of a gurney, wearing a turnout jacket, snow on his helmet.

Owen could have guessed that Darek was a fireman. What

he didn't see coming was the victim on the stretcher, the blonde hair cast over a bloody pillow, a bandage to her head.

"Grace?" His mother spoke the words for him. "What—?" She caught up to the gurney, even as Darek took her arm.

"She's okay, Mom. Hit the windshield, so they're going to do a concussion protocol on her. And head wounds bleed a lot —"

"I'm fine, Mom," Grace said from under the blankets, somewhere in the mess of bandages. "I just—"

"Shh—" said Darek, but Grace pushed his hand away.

"How's Eden?"

Owen walked over to get a better look, and just as Grace was being wheeled in, the curtain in the ER room flung back and Jace stood there, his gaze on Grace.

And behind him, in the bed, wearing a hospital gown and hooked up to an IV, and probably medicine, Eden.

"Grace—what are you doing here?"

"I came to see you." Grace started to sit up, but Darek put a hand on her. "Sorry, sis—"

"Are you okay? How's the baby?" said Grace. They lined her up next to Eden. Jace still held Eden's hand, and to Owen's mind, his countenance hadn't exactly improved.

Someone get the man a chair.

"Still a heartbeat," Eden said quietly, her hand on her belly. "So far so good." She offered a tiny smile.

"How'd it happen?" their father asked as he came up to Darek.

"I don't know. It's a mess. I think she swerved to miss a car at Cutaway Creek and spun out of control. She landed in the ditch, but the car she tried to miss landed in the creek, and the CRT is trying to get to it. I hopped in the ambulance with Grace but the rest of the CRT is there."

His dad turned to his mom. "I should get home and get to plowing."

"I'll go with you, Dad," Owen said. He was no help here, really, and Scotty might need a hand.

His father touched Grace's toe, then walked over to Eden. "Honey. Whatever happens, God is with you." He clamped his hand on Jace's shoulder. "This is not a surprise to Him, right?"

Jace nodded, his mouth a grim line, his hand still in Eden's.

Owen followed his father out of the hospital and they got into the truck. Around them, the wind howled, and ice caked the windshield. His father ran the heater a moment before he got out and scraped the windows.

Got back in. "It's a blow, that's for sure."

"Glad we're not at sea," Owen said. "Last time we had a blizzard at sea, I threw up for three days. Terrifying stuff."

"Your mom told me that you nearly had another man-overboard moment."

His father pulled out onto the road, the snow icing their windshield.

"Yeah. We took on water, and the Coast Guard had to take two trips. But we were fine."

He caught the look his father flashed at him.

"What?"

"Nothing." He reached over, touched his son's leg. "So, do you like it? Living out on the sea? I mean, it's not for everyone. Do you miss shore life?"

Huh. "Dad, I know you and Mom worry. But it's the life Scotty wants. And *I* want what Scotty wants."

"I know it is—"

"I spent most of my life being about me. I can't be that guy. And..." Shoot, but he should probably tell him the truth. "Dad, Scotty and I aren't having kids."

His father glanced at him, frowned. "Really?"

"Yes. So it would help if Mom didn't make any more 'when are you having kids' comments. It's...it only puts a dagger in Scotty's heart."

His father made a sound. Maybe of agreement, but Owen wasn't sure.

"Thanks."

Another sound.

They turned onto the Evergreen resort road and wound their way past the snow-laden trees, toward the gleaming lodge in the woods.

"I need to get changed and head back out with the plow," his father said as they pulled up. Owen got out and came around the truck—

Maybe it was a splotch of ice, maybe just his balance off, maybe even the illness he wouldn't talk about, but even as his father stepped out, his worn work boot whooshed out from under him and suddenly the old man slammed into the ground.

Oof.

"Sheesh, Dad, you okay?" Owen reached out even as his dad groaned, pushed himself up.

"You'd think I'd get used to falling on the ice. We need to get some salt down on the driveway before any of our guests get hurt."

"I'll do that," Owen said, as his father took his hand. Owen helped him the rest of the way up.

His father put a hand to his back. "The doctor said I might be feeling some effects—"

"I knew it!" Owen put his arm around his father's waist. "I *knew* it."

His father looked at him, disentangled himself. "Knew what?"

Owen looked at him. "That you're sick!" He stepped away from him, the cold biting through him. "How bad is it?"

His father just stared at him. Then he closed his mouth. "I'm not sick."

Owen gave him a look.

"Fine. Listen. It's been an issue for a while now, but we wanted to wait to talk to you kids after Christmas—"

"Wow. Dad. Seriously? Don't you think we deserve to know?"

"Well, I guess I thought maybe there were more important things than—"

"Than you telling us that you're not going to be around? That you're dying?"

His father blinked at him. "Son—listen, you don't need to worry."

Didn't need to... Wow. "Dad—listen. I know I live way out in Alaska, but I still care about this family. You and Mom. And I know I don't get home as often as I'd like, but—well, you know the life Scotty and I live, and I thought you supported it."

"We do support you." His father was frowning at him. "I just wanted to make sure that your life is what you wanted—"

"It is. Exactly what I want—but that doesn't mean I don't care. That I don't want to know if you're sick."

"John! Is that you?"

The call came from the front door where Scotty stood. She wore a blanket wrapped around her. "Ingrid called and wants you to call her back."

"Okay, I'll be right in." He pulled out his phone. "Dead."

Owen didn't know why the argument sent a fist into his gut.

Okay, no, it wasn't exactly the life he wanted, but a guy wasn't going to complain when he was almost all the way happy.

Scotty had gone back inside. Owen came in, his father already taking off his boots and outer clothing. He went upstairs, maybe to change into his warmer clothes.

She sat with little Sully's head on her lap, Mace tucked up on the other side of her.

The sight simply jolted him right through, and he couldn't move.

"Hey," he said quietly.

"Hey." She made a face. "They fell asleep here, and I couldn't move them."

"Right. I'll help you." He walked over and pulled Sully into his arms. The boy stirred, then flopped his head against Owen's chest, and again, the jolt went through him.

Breathe. He was just tired. It had nothing to do with his conversation with his father, or the weird, raw afternoon.

He carried Sully up to Jace and Eden's room and tucked him into the lower bunk. Emmie was already asleep in her sleeping bag on the mattress on the floor.

Pulling the covers over him, Owen then went back for Mace.

Scotty followed him up. Stood at the door. "They're so sweet."

"They are. When they're sleeping. But let's not forget the terrors they are when they're awake." He ran his hand over Mace's hair. "I hate to think about the trouble my sons would get into." He gave a mock shiver. Turned. "Dodged a bullet there."

But Scotty just stared at him, her eyes hard. And then they filled. "I can't do this anymore."

She turned away and headed down the stairs.

"Scotty?"

He followed her, but she was already on her way to the den, their bedroom.

He managed to catch her before she shut the door. She was standing with her face to the window, her breath hiccupping. "Scotty?"

"Sorry, Owen. I...I'm just being emotional. I don't know what's come over me lately. It's just..." She turned. Pressed her hands on his chest. "I'm just tired."

"It's been a long day—"

"Of fishing."

He blinked at her. "Oh. I see. Um..."

"I just..." She tugged the blanket around her. "Don't you miss this?"

It was a trap. He knew it. And so he stood, his heart thundering, not sure... "I...I thought that's what you wanted."

"I did, but...I don't know. After the accident..."

"It's an old ship, Scotty. And we're okay—"

"No, we're not, Owen. I'm not okay."

He stared at her.

"I'm...scared. And I don't know why—I just am."

"But—"

"I don't want to be a fisherman anymore."

"What?"

"I heard you out there on the deck telling everyone that you'd like to come back, but I don't believe you."

She met his gaze, and in it he saw the woman who had, once upon a time, been a detective. She folded her arms. "I know you, Owen. First you're a hockey player, and you gave yourself to that. And then your world fell apart, and so did you. And now you're a fisherman, and you've given yourself to that." She put her hands on his chest. "And you're afraid of losing your identity as the family renegade. As the pirate uncle."

He drew in a breath. "I'm not the family handyman. Darek is—"

"But you could be. You just have to see it." Her voice fell. "You're not the prodigal anymore, O. In fact, you could be the hero."

He had nothing. Because even as she stood there, the wind howling behind her, he was the guy lying on the ice, his eye destroyed, his world turning black. And Scotty had given it light again.

But maybe he hadn't seen it fully, even then.

You could be the hero.

A knock at the door, and then his dad stuck his head in.

159

"Sorry. It was open. But um… Do you think you could run the plow for me?"

Owen looked at him, frowned. "I've never driven a plow. Are you sure I can do it?"

"Son. Just drive carefully and follow your headlights. Of course you can do it."

Owen looked at Scotty, who smiled at him and nodded. "Okay." He turned back to his dad. "Yeah."

"Great. We'll leave in a bit—I'll drop you at the city garage on my way back to the hospital."

Owen stilled. "What? Is it Grace?"

His father shook his head, swallowed. "No. They pulled the driver out of the creek, and he just came in." He took a breath. "The driver was Roark."

See, Grace was going to be just fine. Everybody just needed to calm down.

Casper had spotted his sister sitting up on the gurney in the ER as soon as he and Amelia walked into the hospital ER. Beside her stood his mother, looking a little drawn, and Darek, dressed in his DHVFD turnout gear.

But Darek here, at the hospital, told him he didn't have to rush over to the fire station and don his own volunteer fire-fighter gear. The CRT probably had everything under control.

"Sorry I missed all the fun." Casper came in and grabbed his sister's toe. She wore a bandage on her forehead. "Head bumped him, huh? I told you, sis, you gotta pop your head, in and out fast, and the other guy is the one who comes away bloody."

Darek just stared at him. "What is wrong with you?"

But Grace laughed, and that loosened the terrible band in his chest that had tightened with every slow, agonizing mile from his house.

Amelia had walked in after him, and now came up the gurney too. "You had us scared."

"Sorry."

"How'd it happen?" Amelia asked.

"I was on my way to see Eden and everything happened so fast. I could hardly see, except for headlights, and suddenly, they were turning into my lane, and I hit the brakes, but I started sliding, and then out of nowhere another car—I think it was a Caravan—came toward me. I don't think it even had its lights on—but I swerved to avoid it, but so did the car in front of me, and suddenly we were spinning. I think I hit it, but I'm not sure.

A petite woman, wearing a white ski jacket, a little blood on her sleeve, walked into the room and came up to them. "Grace, how are you?"

"Hey, Doc. It seems you can't get rid of me."

A doctor, huh?

"It's clearly a very small town," the doc said. She lifted Grace's wrist, quietly taking her pulse. "Looks like they're taking good care of you," she said, examining the pad over Grace's wound. "Did they do a concussion protocol on you yet?"

"Yes. Mild. I can probably go home tonight, although my car can't."

"Yeah, the accident happened right in front of me and Jake. We saw the car spin and hit Grace's car—and then it slid off the road."

"How's the driver of the other car?"

" It went into the creek."

"Oh no—"

"The emergency response team in town was out there. Jake stayed, but I thought I'd come here and check in on you."

Grace turned to Casper, then Darek. "This is Dr. Aria Silver. She and her husband, Jake, are up here doing some skiing for the week."

"The only snow in Minnesota right now is machine-made," the doc said.

"Until tonight," Darek said.

"How's Max doing?" the doc said.

Grace made a face, shook her head. Dr. Silver nodded. "Well, it was worth a try."

Casper frowned. Worth a try for—oh, wait. The experimental trial.

Wow, how it must tear his sister apart not to be able to fix her husband—or at least try.

"Where's Eden?" Amelia asked Grace.

"The bleeding stopped, but they admitted her for the night to keep an eye on the baby." Grace addressed the doctor. "Eden is my sister, and she's pregnant with a high-risk pregnancy."

"Why is she high risk?" Dr. Silver asked.

"The baby has Down Syndrome and some sort of heart defect."

"Really. Can I talk to her?"

"She's in a room somewhere," Grace said. "She's the one with the husband who looks like a mountain."

Casper grinned. Yes, Jace did look like a mountain.

The doctor squeezed her arm. "You're a trooper, Grace. Glad to see you're okay." She exited, and Casper closed in where she'd left.

"You sure you're okay?" Casper said.

"Yes. I'm fine."

He squeezed her arm. "Okay. I should head back to the house. I have some grout that is drying."

"I can be over to help with painting tomorrow," Darek said as Casper turned.

The ER bay doors opened, just then, letting in a curtain of snow and swirl of frigid air. And four men carrying a Stryker litter. Peter Dahlquist, his cousin Nick, Boone Buckam, their new CRT director, and Jack Stewart, a former Pararescue trooper who also moonlighted as the chef down at the VFW. They carried a man whose leg was splinted, blankets covering the rest of his body.

Except, of course, for his face, which was covered in an oxygen mask, but even through that, recognition sparked in Casper.

Oh. *No.*

Casper moved toward Amelia even as she saw the man, as she cried out. "Roark!"

Casper caught her as she made to run to his side. "Wait a second, honey. Let them get him in." Then he wrapped his arms around her. Her entire body shook as they set the gurney on the empty bed.

"Maybe he should be airlifted to Duluth," Boone said. "He might have internal bleeding—but Jae, our pilot, says it's too rough out to fly."

Jae was the very petite former Army chopper pilot who came in behind them. "Vitals," she said and handed off a clipboard to Colleen Dekker, tonight's ER nurse. "I know it's hard to read—I can't feel my fingers."

They began to strip off Roark's blankets. He too had a facial contusion that ran down from his forehead, but the cold had frozen it, leaving blood on his face, quickly turning sticky. As they rolled back the blankets and cut his clothing, Casper saw the deep bruise across his chest.

"Airbag," said Jack, at Amelia's quick gasp.

Their mother came to stand with Amelia, taking her hand, but Casper continued to hold her. Maybe hold her up, he didn't know, but it was all he could think to do. *Hang in there, sis. Breathe.*

Colleen had taken Roark's vitals, his BP. "Pressure is good—130/70, so he's not going into shock. What's his name?"

"Roark St. John," Amelia said quietly. "My Roark."

Colleen nodded. "Mr. St. John, can you hear me?"

He wore a full mask, so Casper couldn't hear, but he did see him nod, even if he didn't open his eyes.

And that was all Amelia needed. She broke away from Casper—in truth, he let her go—and pushed up to Roark's side opposite the nurse. Took his hand. "Roark, I'm here. I'm so sorry. I'm here." She bent her head down next to his.

Boone, Nick, Peter, and Jack had all moved away and came to stand by Casper.

"How bad was it?"

"He was in the water, half-submerged, but maybe that's what slowed his bleeding," Jack said.

"We had to use the Jaws of Life on the car," said Peter. "Did you get my text?"

"Sorry. Yes, but by the time I saw it Cole told me to come here. It won't happen again."

"It's okay. We had a full turnout. Even had a stranger pitch in." He nodded toward a blond man who stood at the entrance of the door. "Works for some SAR team down in Minneapolis."

The man nodded at Casper, his mouth a grim line.

"I'll get an IV in," Colleen said. "The ER doc is transporting someone to surgery. It's been a busy night."

"John!" His mother moved from Casper's side and he turned to see his father walk in. The guy grimaced as if in pain when she put her arms around him.

Huh. Darek's words from before slammed into his heart, sat down. *Dad is sick.*

"How is he?" his dad asked.

"Who are you?"

"His...father. In law."

Casper glanced at him, but if they wanted information, it sounded like the best answer.

Jack nodded. "Hypothermic, and his leg is in bad shape."

Colleen stepped back and removed her gloves. "IV is in. You just hang tight. It's got morphine in it, so you might be a little groggy." She looked at Amelia. "The ER doc will be here soon."

Casper walked up to Roark. Looked at Amelia. "Okay, sis, I think now's the time to tell him what you told me."

Roark reached with his IV hand and moved his oxygen mask. "What did she tell you?" His words, however, emerged soft and slurred. His eyes closed.

"Are you going to be okay, Ames?" Casper asked.

She drew in a breath, met his gaze. Nodded.

He moved away, but she followed him, grabbed his arm. "Thanks."

"For what?"

Her smile was soft. "For knowing when to hold me up."

Huh. "Sure. Anytime."

She kissed his cheek, then she walked back to Roark, pulling the drape behind her.

Casper turned to Grace. "You need some holding up too?"

"I'll take care of that, thanks, Casp." Max walked into the room, Yulia beside him. She ran over to her mother, her arms around her, crying.

"I'm sorry. I'm so sorry."

Grace held her, also apologizing for whatever had happened between them..

Max gave him a grim-mouthed look. "Coulda been worse."

Casper patted him on the shoulder as he walked out. Much worse.

In fact, they had so much, so very much to be thankful for.

Darek stood there with their parents in the lobby. "Going back to the house?"

Yes. The word almost left his lips, but it clogged in his throat. No. "I'm going home."

Darek nodded. "Me too." He looked at his dad. "Call me if anything changes. Oh, by the way, aren't you supposed to be plowing?"

"Owen's at the wheel."

"It's like you've given him the keys to the Zamboni." Darek shook his head.

"I've never driven the plow," Casper said as he walked out with Darek.

"Owen has all the fun," Darek said. "Drive safe." He lifted his hand.

Casper's truck hadn't even warmed by the time he pulled up to his house. It was dark, just the porch light on, and he tiptoed inside, pulled off his boots and jacket then headed upstairs.

Layla's door was ajar, and he looked in at her, her dark hair on the pillow, clutching a silly bear from her collection. He closed her door to conserve the heat in her room and then went to Rhett's room. He was sleeping on her stomach, his knees pulled up, his bum in the air. Casper pushed him over gently and tucked the covers around him. Kissed his sweaty cheek.

The lights to his bedroom were off, but he didn't need them to pull off his jeans, shirt, and socks and climb into bed. Raina was breathing heavily, but she stirred. He scooted close to her, forming his body around hers, putting his arm around her waist and pulling her close.

She sighed and wove her fingers into his. "What are you doing?"

"What I should have done a long time ago."

"Mmm. What's that?"

"Holding you up." Her hand squeezed in his as the night fell softly around them, untouched by the blizzard roaring outside their flimsy windowpanes.

10

"**A**re you okay?"

Strange that Eden thought she should ask Jace this, but the man still wore a stricken look, even an hour after she'd been admitted to the hospital.

He hadn't looked this way since...well, since a year ago when he had climbed out of frigid waters holding an unbreathing Emmie.

Even after Eden had given her breaths, after Emmie had come back to them, he hadn't spoken for a long, long time.

Now, he appeared just as wrung out, his dark hair askew from his hands running through it as the doctor had run the ultrasound wand over her just-showing belly.

There's a heartbeat, the doc had said, and Eden had wanted to weep with relief.

Jace had sunk down into a chair, his hands folded behind his neck as if he might be putting his head between his knees.

It didn't help that Grace had been wheeled in on a gurney. She couldn't believe the close call on the highway.

Jace looked up at her at the question and nodded, and she didn't believe him for a second.

"She's going to be okay."

He nodded again, but she wasn't sure, then, if he knew who she was talking about. "Our daughter. She's going to be okay."

"It's a girl?"

"That's what the doctor said—Jace, didn't you hear her?"

The contractions had stopped, but if she needed to stay in bed every moment until their daughter was born, she was in. Because as soon as the doctor had shown her their child, she knew...

She *wanted* this baby.

With every heartbeat, she loved this child, for as long as God would let her have her.

Jace was sort of staring through her.

Behind him, the big window that looked out over Deep Haven was dark, and in the reflection, she saw herself in bed, an IV dripping Brethine into her veins, just in case. She wore her hospital gown, but to her eye, she didn't look as distressed or even as overwhelmed as she'd been this morning.

With a start, she realized something had shifted inside her.

Her mother's voice drifted into her head. *God can change your desires...if you are willing to give them to Him.*

It was one thing to say the words.

Quite another to feel them, in her soul.

Yes, yes she wanted this child.

Their daughter.

In fact, "Jace. C'mere."

He frowned, then got up from his chair and walked over to her.

"No. Sit." She patted the bed.

He sat down next to her, taking up almost all the room. But she rolled over on her side and took his hand, weaving her fingers through his. "You're going to need to snap out of it because I need you all here for this baby."

It took a couple blinks for her words to sink in. He nodded. "I'm all here."

"Are you? Because you've been acting pretty strange since we got the news. A little like you've been slammed into the boards and are spinning out on the ice, only with a weird grin on your face."

This tweaked a smile up his face. Then, he sighed and put his other hand over hers, so big it dwarfed hers. Warm. Solid. Present. "Sorry. I just..." He took a breath, then got up. Walked away from her. "I need to tell you something."

She didn't know why a boulder sank into her heart, but a thousand what-ifs flashed through her head. He'd been fired. He didn't want this child. He was leaving her—

No. Stop.

"I've been faking it."

She raised an eyebrow. "Faking...what?"

"This...calm thing you have going on. I wanted it, too, so I thought if I could just...fake it, you know, 'til I made it, everything would be fine, but..." He stuck his hands into his pockets. "I'm not you, Eden. Never have been. I'm completely freaking out about this baby."

She had nothing. "Jace—*I've* been freaking out about this baby."

"No you haven't. You never freak out—okay, occasionally, like when the boys opened all the Christmas presents under the tree a couple weeks ago—"

"Yeah, well, it'll wreck their Christmas—"

"No it won't, but..." He came over to her and sat again on the bed. "I just keep going back to that moment last year when Emmie went through the ice."

"I definitely freaked out."

"No. You stood on the dock waiting for me to find her and..." He looked away. "I nearly didn't, you know. I went down, and she was right there, but was sinking and I grabbed for her hand and I missed. And I thought—'I've lost her.'"

"But you didn't. You got her."

He met her gaze. "But sometimes—a lot of the time—I dream that I didn't. That she slipped through my hands again, and that I came up empty-handed."

She caught his face in her hands. *"But you didn't."*

He let out a breath. "But it really punched me. This idea that I would fail. Her. You. All of us. And now this baby…" He shook his head. "For the last week, I've been under the water, seeing Emmie slip from my grip."

"And pretending you're okay, just like you did when you came out of the water. Except you weren't, because you were hypothermic, and we could have lost you too if Casper hadn't seen that your lips were blue."

"I didn't even notice. I was watching you save our daughter, giving her breaths. I feel like that's what I do—I watch you raise our kids. I come home from days on the road, and somehow you've written another chapter in your book, gone to a school conference, taught Emmie how to bake a cake, attended hockey camp at four a.m. with the boys, and upped your kettlebell reps."

"I wish. My kettlebell is holding down a load of your dress shirts that *you* need to iron." But she smiled. "I don't do all that."

"You do. And you don't even notice it."

"And you don't notice that you come home tired from practice, or the road, just in time for the kids to launch themselves on you, and for you to fall to the carpet to wrestle them. Or that Sully has the best slap shot on his peewee team, and Mace can out-stick anyone on the ice—maybe even his coach."

"His coach can barely skate backward."

"Not to mention that all the kids can spot an icing infraction before the refs do."

"Easy—"

"And somehow, they all make their beds every morning."

"That's pure intimidation and threats."

"But you make it happen. Jace, you're in this game as much as I am. I just happen to be the leading scorer."

"Wow, how I love it when you talk hockey." He leaned down and pressed his forehead to hers. "I love you."

His hand curled behind her neck and she raised her face to his.

Kissing Jace was like being swept up in a wave, carried, overwhelmed, floating...she could lose herself forever in his touch. Her hand pressed his chest, his heartbeat thumping, Oh, how she loved this man. Their children. Their overwhelming, messy, chaotic, beautiful life.

"Eden," he said, a hum deep in his throat. "I thought I was going to lose you." He met her eyes, his so impossibly blue. "I can't lose you."

"You won't, J-Hammer."

He smiled, something slow and a little dangerous, and kissed her again.

Yes, he could bring her to another place, another world when he wanted to.

Except right now, they lived in the real world, and they weren't at home, in their warm bed and...

She pushed on his chest and he lifted his head. Gave her a wry smile. "Sorry. I get a little carried away when we have a moment alone."

He moved his hand then, and touched her belly, over the cotton blanket. "So. What the doctor said. I was a little afraid you...well, I know that you would never say yes, but I felt like you felt—"

"Overwhelmed? Yes. But..."

"Your dad said something to me tonight. Us, really, but... well, that we're not supposed to be able to fix everything. If we were, we wouldn't need God. We wouldn't need Christmas."

"So, what do we do?"

"I don't know. Ask God for a miracle?"

She touched his hand. "This is our miracle, Jace. For as long as we have her. The fact that we need each other to create a life. And not just our children, but our *life*. Team Jacobsen."

He nodded. "Team Jacobsen." He closed his eyes.

"What are you doing?"

"Praying that God will protect our latest draft pick."

Yes.

He opened his eyes. "By the way, do you know Gabe Michaels?"

"Of course. He lives at the Garden. It's a home for people with special needs."

"He helped Sully pet a goat."

She took his hand. "Gabe is a great guy, and if our daughter has Down syndrome, she will be just as amazing."

He nodded, and it seemed something inside him just sort of released, as if he'd been holding his breath.

She grinned. "I know her name."

"Really?" He cocked his head.

"It's Noelle."

"Yeah, it is."

He was bending to kiss her again when a knock came at the door.

"Come in," Eden said and Jace turned.

A petite, dark-haired woman opened the door. She wore a pair of ski pants and a fleece jacket, a hat with a pompom. "Hello. My name is Dr. Aria Silver. I met your sister at a hockey game a few days ago, and—wait." She stopped, looked at Jace. "Are you Jace J-Hammer Jacobsen?"

"Nice to meet you, Doc."

"Wow. You're even bigger in person."

Jace laughed.

"You should see him on skates," Eden said.

"I have. I miss you out on the ice, but I love seeing you coach the Blue Ox. I'm a huge fan."

"Thanks."

"Do you know Sam Newton and his daughter, Maddy?"

"Yeah. We're good friends. He runs—"

"Sammy's Bar and Grill, in St. Paul. Your picture is on the wall."

"He's got dozens of team pictures from his years playing hockey. How do you know Sam?"

"Actually, I know Maddy. Olivia, her stepmom, and I are good friends."

"Wow, that's a crazy small world. What are you doing here?"

"My husband, Jake, and I are up for the holiday, visiting friends and skiing. He and his friend Ham were playing in the pickup game on Friday when Max fell. That's when I met Grace —and then tonight we happened to be driving home from the resort when we came upon the accident. Talk about a small town—anyway, I came in to check on her and she mentioned that you had a little one who needed some help."

Eden looked at her. "What kind of doctor did you say you were?"

"A double board-certified pediatric cardiothoracic surgeon."

"What?" Eden said. "You're a heart doctor?"

"I was Maddy's heart transplant doc. Both times. Such a fighter." She pulled up a chair. "I'll need to see your charts and run my own tests, but have you ever heard of an in-utero balloon atrial septoplasty?"

"Nope," said Eden. She reached out and took Jace's hand. "But it sounds like a miracle to me."

Roark was going to die and Amelia would never get to tell him Yes. No, rather I Do.

The thought consumed her as she stood in his tiny room, the one where they'd taken him from her an hour ago to set his leg and do an ultrasound for internal bleeding and any other injuries.

She glanced at the clock. No, more than an hour ago.

Amelia wrapped her arms around herself, the blizzard outside angry, wild, the wind banging against the panes of the hospital as if it wanted in.

The ferocity of it all shook her through.

What if it was too late? What if, despite his accident, he still didn't want her? He'd fallen asleep, only squeezing her hand after Colleen had given him the pain meds and...

She pressed her fingers to her eyes. Calm. Down.

Like Casper said—Roark had chased her around the globe. Sure, it was his family's organization that funded their projects, but she'd been the one to believe, to hear, to follow God's call on her heart to be a missionary.

And sure, Roark had eventually heard it too, maybe always had, but she was the one who kept charting out new schools or orphanages around the world. She could probably do without the few close calls she had with the black mambas, men wielding machetes, and the lack of water and internet, but...she loved how her heart felt when she walked into someone's life with hope. When she saw that hope change them.

And Roark was right there, all the time, to share that with her.

Wow, she loved him.

He was her partner in every way except the most important.

Yes, Roark, it's time for I Do.

Unless she was too late.

Please, God.

"Ames? You okay?"

The voice stilled her, and she turned. Gaped.

Seth Turnquist, her former flame, now husband to her best

friend, Ree, stood in the doorway to Roark's room, wearing a pair of jeans, a parka, and a snow-dusted hat.

As if he might be a buddy stopping by to visit his old pal Roark.

Weird.

"Hi. Seth."

"Is Roark...he's okay, right?" Seth came into the room. He was a big man. A lumberjack, in every sense of the word, with his blond hair, broad shoulders, but oh-so-gentle way about him. A gentle giant, except, of course, when he was fighting fires. Because after she'd broken his heart, he'd fled out west to be a wildland hot shot and she'd tried, unsuccessfully, not to blame herself.

She'd wept with joy when he'd married Ree two weeks ago. Now, a crazy relief, a wave of affection swept over her.

"I don't know," she said softly. And then the tears came.

"Oh, Ames," he said and came into the room, his arms open.

She stepped into them, wrapping her arms around him, her head against his chest.

Nothing but a sweet memory of being the girl he'd once loved. He could have been her happily ever after. Except Roark had won her heart.

And God had always had something better, someone better, for Seth.

Of course.

"He's going to be fine," Seth said, his chin on her head. "And you two are going to get married and live happily ever after."

She let out a sound that was ridiculously stupid, terribly wretched, and had Seth pulling away from her. "What?"

"I just...Roark broke up with me. He was on his way out of town."

Seth just stared at her. "Really."

"Yes. Because...we're still not married, if you hadn't noticed."

He lifted a shoulder. "I noticed." He offered a half smile. "I didn't want to ask."

She wiped her cheek. "He told me that...well, he compared himself to you."

"He's hardly me, sweetheart." He gave her a look.

She laughed. "Okay, calm down. He just meant that...that I had led you on."

He raised an eyebrow and maybe she shouldn't have told him that.

"I didn't—or at least, I didn't mean to, by the way."

"I know...I think. I guess it might have felt that way at the time. I was really crazy about you, Ames."

"Yeah."

"But, see, once I got my head clear, I realized...well, that God had someone else for me, and Ree—she's *the one*, you know?"

"I do. Yes. And I'm so happy for you two—"

"But if I had married you, you would have always wondered, right? If you'd done the right thing? And so would I. With Ree, I know she wants me. And I want her. And that's how it should be, right?"

She nodded. "I do want Roark. He's...*the one*."

Seth smiled. "So, what's the holdup?"

"I was afraid of losing the life I had, losing myself, I think, and got scared."

He folded his hands across his chest. "Aw, Ames. Do you not know yourself at all? You're the bravest person I know. And, if you get lost, Roark is the guy who is going to find you, right?" He winked.

And her mind went back to the terrible accident so many years ago where she'd fallen in a ravine and Roark hadn't given up.

In fact, in the ravine, God had shown her not only the snapshots of her life that brought her to, well, the ravine, but also allowed her to look up, see the stars, the heavens, the mighty hand of God in all of it.

And in the end, God had shown Roark where to find her.

Because she'd never been lost at all.

The door opened to the room and an orderly held it open.

Roark looked as if he'd been trapped under a car and dragged. A cast wrapped his leg from his foot to above his knee, and his upper chest was taped, with a tube that ran out of his body. A butterfly bandage covered the cut over his eye. An oxygen cannula was fixed under his nose.

"Roark?" Amelia walked over to him.

"He's groggy, but he should be coming out of it soon," said the nurse.

But even as she stood there, he reached out his hand from under the covers. Opened it.

She folded hers into it.

He squeezed.

She bent her head, tears burning her eyes.

Seth walked around the bed, taking the place the nurse had vacated. "C'mon, tough guy. Wake up."

Roark roused to his words.

Huh.

Seth grinned. "See. I think we're going to be friends."

Roark inhaled, his eyes opening. He stared at her, blinking, as if piecing together his world.

"Hey," she said. "You're in the hospital. Ran off the road."

He nodded, then glanced at Seth. Frowned. Seth leaned down to him. "You gotta stop trying so hard to get the girl. You won, pal." Then he stood, reached out and touched Amelia's arm. "Make good choices," he said to Amelia.

"Thanks, Seth," she said softly.

He left and she turned to Roark. He was watching her, those blue eyes searching hers. "Are you in pain?"

"You're here."

"Of course I'm here."

He swallowed, then closed his eyes. "Amelia—"

"Me first." She took a breath. "You'll never be Seth."

His eyes opened.

"You're the one, Roark. The one I will love forever. But I can see why you compared yourself to him. I was afraid that because of everything you've gone through—and all the things we've seen—that you would want us to come home and stop... well, doing what we do. So...I kept putting you off."

He was watching her, and now swallowed, nodded. "Just like Seth, you thought I had our lives all planned out, without asking you."

"Yes." She drew in a breath. "Do you?"

He coughed, then winced. "No. I just...my only goal is to marry you. I figured that we'd figure out the rest together."

She bent and put her head on his forehead. "I don't want to say it, but maybe I'm glad you didn't make it out of town."

"I was turning around, Ames."

She lifted her head. "You were?"

"I know what I said, and I almost believed myself. And then I stopped at a gas station just outside town and met these guys in a Caravan, and they were lost, and right then, I knew if I left you, I would be too." He touched her face, his warm hand on her cheek. "You have always been a sort of light for me, Ames, and without you...all I could see was darkness."

He coughed again, made a face. "I drove another ten miles before I got my head together and turned around. That's when I lost control of the car—I've never really driven in snow, and I might have been in a hurry to get back and—suddenly this car came out of nowhere. I think it might have been that Caravan, but I swerved and I think I hit the car behind me. Then everything went black and cold and I was in the river, hurt and stuck. And all I could think was...God, don't let me die before I tell her that I love her. That I will love you on your terms..." His eyes filled. "Even if you never marry me. My dreams are your dreams, Ames. Whatever they are."

"I will marry you, Roark. Right now, tonight, tomorrow—I will marry you."

He coughed again, and his voice turned hoarse. "Really?"

"Mmhmm." She leaned in, her mouth close to his. "How about as soon as you get out of this hospital?"

"Tell the nurse I'm ready to be discharged," he whispered against her lips.

Then he kissed her, something short, tender, sweet, but in her memory, she was in Africa, under the stars, in his strong arms as he kissed her good night.

Good, good night.

She lifted her head. "In fact, I think I even know where we can have the ceremony."

"Perfect." He smiled.

Then he coughed again, harder, and his entire body convulsed. Blood splattered out of his lips, onto his blanket, even as his head rolled back. His entire body seized.

"Nurse!" Amelia shouted.

Across the bed, the heart monitor turned erratic.

On the bed, his body collapsed.

The monitor shrilled as the line went flat.

"Code Blue!" Colleen Decker charged into the room, two other nurses behind her. She lowered Roark's bed even as she looked at Amelia. "Go. Now. So we can save his life."

11

F or Amelia, the service had to be perfect.

A commemoration of their life together, of their dreams and hopes. Roark's uncle Donovan was coming, of course, so at least someone would be here to share his stories.

Grace stood in front of a table of pictures she'd managed to pull from Amelia's Facebook page, a collage of events over the past six years. Amelia and Roark in front of a castle in Old Prague, and another shot of them in Deep Haven, sometime after he'd proposed.

More shots—in Uganda, at Hope Orphanage, and at a school in the Ivory Coast, and the refugee school in Nigeria. Always with Roark, his arm around Amelia, behind her, stalwart, a tiny smile playing on his handsome face.

No wonder Amelia had fallen for him.

Grace set a vase of faux flowers on the table—a bouquet she borrowed from Megan Barrett, their local event planner.

"There's a timer beeping in the kitchen." Raina had come out into the living room of her and Casper's beautiful newly remodeled home. The perfect venue for their private ceremony.

Private, perfect, and of course, unexpected.

Emotion clogged Grace's throat as she followed Raina to the kitchen.

So much had happened over the past four days, she'd been able to keep ahead of the rush of, well, all of it.

Yulia stood at the oven door, now open, wearing a couple oven mitts, pulling out the salmon puffs. "These look perfect, Mom."

Something had shifted between them since that moment in the hospital when Yulia had clung to her, weeping.

So much more weeping than Grace had expected. Sure, they'd gotten into fights before, but...

Mom, please don't die.

Yulia's broken voice rushed back to her. *I'm sorry, I'm so sorry.*

No, it was Grace who was sorry, and she said so. But Yulia had kept weeping until Max finally pulled her away, holding her.

And she'd clung to him too.

That's when Max looked at her over the top of Yulia's head with his own broken look and met Grace's eyes. Took a breath. Then maneuvered Yulia away so he could meet her eyes. "We will not leave you, honey, I promise."

"You can't promise that!" She looked at Max, then Grace. "Mom was nearly killed tonight! And you...*Dad*..." She put her hands over her face, her shoulders shaking.

Max took her wrists and pulled them away.

"Okay, okay, shh. I know. But here's the truth, Yulia. You are safe. You are loved. And you are not alone. You belong to us and Inga and Pops and the family—and God. You are His daughter. Your story is safety. It's family. It's salvation. And it has a happy ending. Your story might have started out rough, but it ends in joy."

Their story ended in *joy.*

Grace nearly burst into tears then, too, because she saw it all.

Walking with Max, hand in hand, on his journey home, building a life of love, he is embedded in the memories, trusting in the promises of heaven.

Because of Christmas.

Because though the Christmas story started rough, it ended in joy.

And today, they'd end Roark's story with joy.

And begin a new one with hope.

Yulia set the tray of puffs on the massive center island in Casper's new home, next to a bowl of sweet corn and crab vinaigrette salad.

And at the end of the island, Eden put the topper, a bouquet of faux poinsettias, on the cake.

A beautiful, two-tiered white wedding cake that just might be Grace's best creation to date. She'd been up most of the night crafting it, but everything had to be perfect.

After all, Roark had waged war with a collapsed lung and a pulmonary clot to win the day. And it helped that the hospital not only had a trauma nurse, but a cardiothoracic surgeon in the building.

Talk about drama in the story.

"Do I need to baste this brisket?" Raina was whisking the barbecue sauce. She wore an apron over her red dress, her dark hair up, and frankly, looked a little overwhelmed in her massive gourmet kitchen. Not that she couldn't keep up, but clearly Casper had gone over the top.

"Not yet. Fifteen more minutes."

Grace hadn't realized that it was Raina's first time seeing the kitchen until they walked in four days ago to the finished house with Raina, who had stood transfixed at the remodel. *Casper... this is beautiful.*

Aw, her brother, who had spent the past twenty-four hours moving in furniture and cleaning up his building project, had actually blushed.

Sweet.

Grace had left them for a long moment while she unpacked her catering supplies and figured where and how they were going to feed their family and a handful of close friends for a sit-down dinner.

On the eve of Christmas Eve, no less.

Raina had toured the house, and then she, Grace, Eden, Amelia, Scotty, and their mother had spent the day decorating.

The front room held the tall Christmas tree that Casper and the guys found on resort property. Eden had crafted a garland from the shorn branches and woven it up the banister. And Amelia had created centerpieces for the three tables and for the altar in the front of the main room—an arch that Darek had built with canoe paddles.

Darek had spray-painted the paddles white, affixed them together, and Amelia had draped them with boughs, ribbon, and tulle. With candles flickering at the windows and a fire in the hearth, it would be the perfect ambiance.

Although, frankly, Roark had suggested getting married in the hospital, so probably he wouldn't care.

Grace lifted the lid on the boiling potatoes. Stuck her fork into one and pressed it against the edge. "Almost done. Yes, baste the brisket."

Yulia was sliding the puffs to a cooling rack when Emmie came into the room. She was dressed in her Christmas best—a red velvet dress that Inga had made for her. Joy and Layla had matching dresses.

"Mom, Inga needs you," Emmie said.

Something had changed in Eden, too, over the past four days. A confidence, or maybe just a peace. Yes, the conversation with Dr. Silver helped—her pioneering surgery just might buy baby Noelle enough time out of the womb for her heart to be strong enough for the major surgery she'd need.

But it was more than that. A sense of confidence, even as she sent her boys out to play in the snow with Jace while she helped alter their mother's wedding dress for Amelia.

"What's going on? A wedding dress catastrophe?" Eden was all smiles as she wiped her hands and pulled off her apron.

"No. Auntie Amelia is missing!"

Everyone stopped—Raina, standing over the open brisket in the oven, the steam rising out of it. Yulia, now chopping tomatoes for the salad. Scotty, who couldn't, suddenly, stand the smell of food and had assigned herself to setting the tables, paused in the kitchen with a handful of silverware. And Grace, who closed the lid to the pot of potatoes as it boiled on the stove.

"Missing?" Grace said.

"Yes. Inga says she's not in her room—"

"She's locked in the bathroom and won't come out." Her mother appeared behind Emmie. She wore a red scoop necked dress, her blonde hair back in a black velvet headband.

"I'm on it," Eden said, and glanced at Grace.

Yep.

They'd turned Raina and Casper's bedroom into the bridal suite, and now Eden knocked on the door to the en suite bathroom. "Ames? What's going on?"

"Please don't tell me you're destroying that makeup we worked so hard on," Grace said, and Eden gave her a look.

"What? I'm just saying, we're running out of time here. The potatoes are almost ready."

Eden shook her head. "Amelia. Please tell me you're not getting cold feet."

Silence.

Grace made a face. "Should I get Jace to break the door in—"

Amelia turned the lock and flung open the door. "No. Just…"

"Aw, you did destroy the makeup," Grace said, and pushed her way into the room. Mascara ran down Amelia's face. "What's with the waterworks?"

Eden too had entered the room. "Ames. What's going on?"

Grace pushed Amelia down on the closed toilet. Took her chin. "It's not too bad. We just need a little cleanup in aisle two."

Eden rolled her eyes.

"I don't know what to say, and I'm going to wreck everything," Amelia said.

Eden folded her arms. "I don't think—"

"Roark always says the perfect thing, in his perfect accent, and I...I don't know what to say."

"How about 'I Do'?" Grace had wet a washcloth and now tipped up Amelia's chin.

"No. I mean for my vows. He's writing his. I...have nothing." She lifted a piece of paper and handed it to Eden.

Eden looked at it. "This is blank."

"My point."

Grace had cleaned off the mascara from Amelia's cheeks and now ran a cotton swab under her eyes. "We'll get this cleaned up in no time."

"It won't matter if I don't have anything to say."

"Okay, sweetie, this is not hard." Eden took the pen from Amelia's hand.

"That's easy for you to say. You're the writer."

"You don't have to be a writer to say what's in your heart."

"It helps."

"Ames. You're a photographer. What do you see when you look at Roark? Imagine you're framing the shot."

She stared at her.

"Look up," Grace said.

Amelia obeyed. "Okay, so there's this one picture of him that I have. He's sitting on the ground, his sleeves rolled up, and he's really dirty. He's been digging a well all day, but now he's playing with this kid. Maybe six years old. They've made a mancala board in the sand, and he's using rocks for his pieces. And the kid is squatting next to him, and he's laughing. I'm not sure what Roark said to him, but I have dozens of pictures just like that—Roark, wearing the work of the day, hanging out with kids, or even adults, and they're...joyful. He has this way of fitting into the world of other people, making them feel safe and accepted and...as if everything is going to be okay, you know?"

Eden was writing.

"Now look down," Grace said and applied mascara to the top lashes.

"What are you writing?"

"Listen. You gotta stop over-thinking stuff. Your vows are easy." She handed the paper to Amelia.

Amelia looked down and smiled.

"What do they say?" Grace asked.

"You'll have to wait." She looked at Eden. "They're perfect."

"My job here is finished. I have sons to find and dress."

Grace added fresh eyeliner, then shadow. "Okay. You're free to put on that dress. No more crying." She took Amelia's hands. "Eden's right. Stop overthinking everything. Just...enjoy, okay?"

Grace's own words settled inside her an hour later as she stood at the top of the stairs, watching Roark hobble up to the altar on his crutches.

He was the best-dressed man in the room, despite his injuries. He had gotten a haircut, shaved, and his uncle Donovan had brought him a tuxedo.

Darek stood beside him, his best man of course, the brother who had helped him become a lumberjack for a day, to win Amelia's heart.

But he'd had it long before then.

Pastor Dan stood at the paddle-arch altar, armed with the marriage license that Ivy was able to certify double time, and on the bride's side were Ree and Seth, Vivien and Boone, Amelia's childhood friends along with nearly everyone else, although Casper and Raina sat on the groom's side, because really, it didn't matter.

Emma Hueston played "Silent Night" on the keyboard set up near the bottom of the stairs, the song winding up and filling the house with beauty.

All is calm. All is bright.

Yes. Yes it was.

Grace just had to stop overthinking everything.

Believe.

Hope.

Enjoy.

She spotted Max sitting with Yulia, who was dressed in a long white and red skirt Inga had made for her. She held her father's hand. And, oh, Max. He'd never looked so handsome, with that long dark hair, trimmed whiskers, that smile that he trained on her when he came into the house.

Thankfully, Owen had been out for the past two days, plowing the roads as the snow continued to fall. Outside a thick blanket of snow frosted the ground, sparkling and silver under a glorious spray of starlight.

"Ready?" Grace turned to Amelia standing at the top of the stairs. Her little sister was stunning, her auburn hair piled up on her head, strands corkscrewing down around her face. Their mother's gown had been refitted and resewn, the puffy arms removed, along with the lacy insert and high neck. Now, embroidered straps fell off her shoulders, and a red velvet sash circled her waist.

Eden had removed the crown attached to her mother's veil and sewn in a comb so that the gauzy veil fell from below Amelia's bun.

Amelia hooked her hand over their father's arm. He wore a black suit, not as fancy as Roark's, but still handsome. "Ready."

Grace nodded at her mother, who stood up, and Amelia descended the stairs on her father's arm, as Emma transitioned to "O Holy Night."

Indeed.

Especially with the look on Roark's face as Amelia met him at the altar. He'd handed off one of his crutches to Darek and took her hand.

Grace slid in beside Max and worked her fingers between his.

Pastor Dan kept it short. Sweet. Beautiful.

Roark spoke his vows as if he'd had them memorized for years. "Amelia, six years ago, you awakened inside of me the man I'd always wanted to be. Your bravery, passion, and desire to reach out to a hurting world humbles me. And it reminds me every day that I am a blessed man to walk this life with you."

Grace looked at Max, and he met her gaze and maybe he was remembering their own vows, spoken on a beach in Cancun. Yes, so blessed.

Amelia pulled out her vows.

Swallowed.

"Roark. Thank you for waiting for me." Then she looked at her paper. "You are my wish come true. My happy ending. Thank you for not giving up when my brothers tried to scare you away."

Snickers, and Darek fist bumped Jace.

Oh brother.

"You make me feel safe. Loved. And when I look at you, I know everything will be okay, no matter where we are. I trust you."

Grace glanced at Eden, who was leaning on Jace's rather large shoulder.

Good job, sis.

Pastor Dan turned to Roark and started on the promises. "Do you, Roark St. John, take Amelia Christiansen to have and to hold…"

Grace looked at Max.

"From this day forward, for better or for worse."

Yes.

"For richer, for poorer…"

Yes

"In sickness and in health."

She squeezed Max's hand.

He looked down at her.

"To love and to cherish."

He bent down, his lips close to her ear. "From this day forward, until death do us part?"

She nodded. He grinned at her, while up at the altar, Pastor Dan repeated the list for Amelia.

Again, Max put his mouth to her ear. "I signed up for the study."

Grace stilled. Looked at him. "What?"

He nodded. "Babe. The thought of losing you made me realize how you—and Yulia—felt." He sighed. "If you need me to fight, I'll fight."

Her eyes filled as the pastor announced Roark and Amelia husband and wife.

"You may kiss your bride."

Max smiled.

And then he did.

"I really feel like this is a bad Christmas Eve tradition." Darek shivered, his entire body frozen as he stood outside, bundled to the teeth, dressed in his Joseph costume. "This is an activity meant for someone who lives in Florida."

"Oh, stop. Think of all the children who are coming to see the animals. Besides, it's not a bad thing to remember the challenges of Mary and Joseph and how God provided for them."

"I'd like God to provide some warm soup and a crackling fire," Darek said, even as he smiled and nodded to Megan and Cole Barrett and their son Josh. He was growing into quite a hockey player, especially under Tiger's coaching. He hadn't yet told his son that they were moving and wasn't looking forward to it.

Frankly, despite his words to Ivy, Darek hadn't made the decision, fully, until the wedding.

Until he realized all that he had with Ivy, how she, too, had met a broken, angry man and changed him. And kept changing him, every day.

He would also follow her anywhere. But better, maybe, to lead them. To make the decision not in acquiescence to his wife's dreams, but making a way for them, fueling them, tending them, making them his own.

Now, to tell his father that he was leaving. Whether they sold the resort or not was up to his father.

"Your mom doesn't expect us for another hour. Remember, they did this years ago."

"Yes. The year Romeo came to live with us."

"How is your cousin?"

"Last I heard he was jumping fire in Montana, or maybe Alaska, with the Jude County Smoke Jumpers."

"Your old outfit. Is Jed Ransom still in charge?"

"I think he retired. You probably don't remember Tucker Newman, but he was a kid who grew up in Deep Haven. He took over for Jed a few years ago."

"Small world."

"I think Tucker met Jed when we had our epic fire that burned down the resort, so not so small."

A breeze lifted snow from the alcove where they'd dug out the manger scene, stirred snowflakes into the night.

"By the way, I'm telling my dad tonight we're leaving."

She looked at him, drew in a breath.

"It's going to be okay, Ivy, I just know it in my bones."

"What, did you get visited by an angel or something?"

"Or something." He grinned. "Actually, it was Max's

announcement that he'd applied for the study. He's not accepted yet, but they're hoping. Apparently, the deadline was a few days ago."

"The study sounds a little rough."

"But it might slow down the disease. I talked to Max afterward and he said that he wants to give Grace and Yulia all the life he can. And so do I, Ivy. So, my choice—we're moving—"

"But—"

"Nope. I know we'll miss the resort, but I've seen Tiger on skates—he's every bit as good as Owen. But the last thing I'll do is send him away to Juniors or somewhere else, alone. And Joy can spend summers here with Layla and Emmie and as long as our family is together, she'll be fine."

Ivy looked up at him, and he couldn't help it. He leaned down and kissed her.

"Hey! Joseph isn't supposed to kiss Mary!" This from Tiago. Peter Dahlquist stood with him, laughing.

"Joseph gets to kiss his wife," Darek growled.

"I think this live Nativity might be a little too live," said Ronnie, Peter's girlfriend.

"All you voyeurs, this show closes in five minutes. Pet your goats and sheep and be off!"

"Wow. I've never met such a grumpy Joseph," said Nick, Peter's cousin. He walked by with his girlfriend, the petite chopper pilot for Deep Haven's CRT. Or at least Darek assumed it was her—he couldn't exactly see her in her massive down parka.

"Merry Christmas," Ivy said, waving.

"C'mon, Mary, it's time to get out of Bethlehem." Darek held out his hand.

"I fear we'll be remembered as the crabbiest holy family ever."

"Better that than the ones that froze to death. Tig! We're heading out!"

Thankfully, Lena, the vet, had stayed to watch the animals as the children petted them and began to round them up. Darek unplugged the lights on the display, plunging them into darkness.

Overhead, the stars shone, casting down a display of glory.

"Which one is the Bethlehem star?" Tiger asked as he crunched through the snow toward them.

Darek found the brightest one in the sky. Pointed.

Yes, he'd miss this view too.

But there were stars in Duluth and wherever God led them.

"Let's go. I'll bet your grandma already has the soup ready."

A half hour later, the smell of the clam chowder greeted him as the family piled inside the entryway. Perry Como sang "(There's No Place Like) Home for the Holidays," and Owen clearly agreed, by the looks of him as he finished up the puzzle. He drank eggnog and was dressed in a crazy Christmas sweater with a tree and holiday lights that actually glowed.

In the kitchen, his mother was stirring the soup while Eden cut the rolls and Raina made sandwiches. Raina seemed different after the wedding. Smiled more.

Maybe they all did. Seeing Amelia marry the man who'd chased her across the ocean, twice, who'd never given up on her, had stirred up memories.

He'd seen more than Max and Grace kissing in the audience.

Had met Ivy's gaze with his own promises.

Now, Amelia and Roark sat on the sofa. They'd stayed last night at Casper's house, while Casper and Raina went back to their bungalow.

They were reading something on his phone.

Roark's uncle Donovan, from across the pond, was chatting with his father near the fire. And the girls were playing with—

"Eden, is that your old dollhouse?"

Eden nodded. "Mom decided to fix it up for the girls, when they're here."

"Hello the house!"

Darek turned and Max, Grace, and Yulia came in. Grace carried a plate of frosted gingerbread men. He took it from her as she peeled off her layers.

"Hey, Max. Any news?"

Max shook his head.

Oh.

Darek carried the cookies into the kitchen. Already Joy had joined her cousins at the dollhouse. And Tiger went to the puzzle table.

He set the cookies on the counter. Took a breath.

Glanced at Ivy, who had grabbed some plates and was setting the table.

Now seemed as good a time as any. He'd already told Tiger and Joy in the car, and they'd handled it with the mixed reviews he'd expected.

Besides, his brothers already knew the truth.

"I have an announcement," Darek said.

Ivy's expression flashed to panic, but he ignored her.

"Dad. Ivy and I and the kiddos are moving to Duluth. She's been appointed to a judgeship and—"

"And it's an opportunity you can't pass up," his father said. He came over from where he'd been standing by the tree. "I know. I agree. I'm so excited for both of you."

Darek blinked at him. "Wait. How did you—did you hear me talking on the deck?"

His father frowned, then looked at Mom. "No. Uh—"

"Noelle Hueston overheard Grace and Ivy talking about it in the bleachers a few days ago," her mother said. "She thought we already knew." Her mother wore an apology in her expression. "Sorry. We didn't want to tell you we knew—we didn't know what you were going to do, and we didn't want to pressure you."

He stared at her, then at his dad. "You're okay with this?"

"Of course, son."

"But who will you get to help? I asked Owen and Casper—"

"Hey," said Casper. "Don't throw me under that bus. You're the resort boss, not me."

"I have a boat," said Owen.

"Yeah," said Sully, coming over to jump on Owen. "He's a pirate!"

Owen caught him, swung him around, and set him on the floor, his hand tickling his tummy. Sully rolled around in giggles.

Darek just stared at his dad. "But what about…" He drew in a breath, met Owen's gaze.

His brother lifted a shoulder.

"What about your illness?"

The entire room went quiet. Ivy's mouth pursed, and Owen endured a jump from Mace without tickling him, just setting him down. Casper ran a hand across his mouth, looked away.

Scotty had come out of the bathroom, and now walked over to Owen, taking his hand.

"What illness, son?" his father said.

"The one you won't tell us about," Owen said. "The one you've been dealing with for a while…remember?"

His father's mouth opened. "Oh. Um—"

"I really can't believe you've been sick all this time and haven't told us," Casper said. "We're your family. You can't just keep things to yourself. You have to let us, at least…show up for you."

"Oh, honey," their mother said. "You show up. You all show up. I mean, look, you're all here for Christmas. Even Owen and Scotty."

"Because I called them," Amelia said. "I heard you and Dad talking, saying you didn't want to tell us until after Christmas. But you were afraid that Dad might be *gone* by then. Gone? What does that even mean?"

"Oh," her father said, and then he looked at their mom and…

Laughed.

And she too put a hand to her mouth. Shook her head.

"What? I don't think this is funny at all," said Eden. "Mom, if something is wrong with Dad—or you—we need to know about it. You're getting older, and—"

"We're not that old, Eden. But thank you," their mother said.

His dad smiled, looking down at his eggnog. "Well, kids, we clearly can't get anything past you. And yes, you deserve to know. But I was going to wait until after Christmas to tell you because, well, I wanted to make sure everything was in place—"

"Before, what? You had to go to Mayo to get your cancer treatments?" Amelia said.

"Calm down," their father said, holding up his hand. "I don't have cancer. Or any other disease. Okay, that's not true." He looked at Darek. "I have a touch of arthritis."

"Arthritis?" Darek said.

"That's what you're suffering with?" Owen said.

"Hey. It's not fun to get old."

Owen shook his head. "So that's what that trip to Mayo was about?"

"Uh, not exactly." He glanced again at Ingrid. "Kids, your mom and I have purchased a boat."

He paused, and in the silence apparently didn't get the response he'd hoped for. He raised an eyebrow.

"Dad. A boat. Big deal. We live on a lake. We could probably use a new boat," Darek said.

"She's a 42-foot monohull sailboat capable of blue-water cruising around the world." And he smiled.

Oh.

In the silence, his mother walked over and took Darek's hand. "Your father needs to be somewhere warmer in the winter. His old bones need the sun, and during our last trip to Florida, we visited Noelle and Eli and...well, they took us to a boat show."

Darek looked around the room. Met Casper's gaze, then Owen's.

Then turned back to his dad. "Just who, Dad, did you expect would run the resort?"

"Well, you, son. But I wasn't going to leave you alone. I have backup."

"Backup."

"Yeah. And..." His father looked at his watch. "He should be here."

"He texted about two hours ago from Duluth," Ingrid said.

"You were just going to *leave*," Darek said.

"Not forever. But yes." He looked at Owen then. "I was thinking that maybe Owen and Scotty might join us. At least in the summer, when their crabbing season is over."

Scotty had wound her fingers through Owen's hand. She looked up at him. "We'd love to, except..." She looked at Ingrid and smiled. "We told you that you'd be the first to know."

"First to know...what?" Owen said slowly.

She smiled, then pulled out a small plastic stick from her pocket. "Three tests, same answer."

Darek wasn't a crying man, but in that moment, even he choked up watching the truth wash over Owen's face.

"You're pregnant?"

"We're pregnant," Scotty said carefully. "What do you think?"

He caught her face, met her eyes. "I think Merry Christmas." And then he kissed her.

Darek caught Ivy's eye, and she was grinning. Crying, but grinning.

Okay, so this was well and good— "Congrats, bro"—but who was going to tend the resort?

Or maybe this *was* the end. Maybe they were really selling. He drew in a breath. Well, they'd all survive. Really.

Evergreen Resort didn't always have to belong to the Christiansens.

Owen let his wife go. "But what about the boat? Alaska?"

"I was thinking maybe Deep Haven would be a great place to grow up."

Owen touched her forehead. "Yeah, it would be. It is." But he looked at his dad. "I don't think I can run this resort alone."

Behind them, the entry door opened, and a swirl of cold air swept into the room. "Wow, Aunt Ingrid, that soup smells amazing."

Darek turned. Seriously? "Romeo?"

"Hey, Dare!" Romeo Christiansen—okay, he wasn't a Christiansen, technically, being a cousin on his mother's side, but Darek had started to think of him that way after he'd lived with them so many years ago. Romeo had gotten the tall genes and had broadened out with the hard work of his firefighting career. He wore a green army jacket, his dark hair long and tied back under a wool hat and carried an army duffle over his shoulder. He let it fall, then walked forward and embraced Darek.

He'd come so far from the angry, reserved teenager he'd been so many years ago.

"Romeo!" his father said and pulled the man into his embrace. "You got my letter."

"Yeah. I was in Montana, trying to figure out what to do for the winter, and thought, hey, I need a change. So yeah, Uncle John, I'll be glad to help you with the resort."

"Atta boy."

Darek just stared at him.

Oh. Romeo was his replacement?

He tried not to let it sting. Except, his gaze went to Owen, and the crazy grin he wore and...

Yes. It was time to pass the proverbial keys to Owen. Let him grow the family he deserved here.

And Romeo, too, who had found refuge here, once upon a Christmas.

"So, Dad, when are you leaving for your big trip?" Casper said, coming over to greet Romeo.

"I enrolled in a two-week sailing course right after the New Year. Which is why I will be gone... Your mom is flying down a few weeks later to join me."

"After Eden and baby Noelle's surgery." Mom had returned to the soup and now put her arm around her daughter. "For as long as they need. John can just tie up the boat and wait for me."

"In the sun. With a glass of lemonade with a little umbrella in it."

Laughter, and even Darek smiled.

Fine. So they might just survive.

"Anyone hungry?" His mother poured the soup into the Christmas tureen, and everyone headed to the table, now extended and added onto with a couple cardboard tables.

"We're at the big table," Sully said as he sat down.

"Please, don't spill," Eden said.

"I got this," Jace said and sat between the boys. He winked at her. She sat down between Mace and Emmie, who held her grandpa's hand.

Casper held Rhett and Sully reached out for baby Rhett's wet paw.

Raina took Casper's hand, then Layla's. And on the other side of Layla sat Owen, who also took her hand, then looked at Casper, who grinned at him.

Next to Casper, Amelia took his hand, and then Roark's, who held onto Sully's.

Scotty reached for her mother-in-law's hand on the other side of her, who held Romeo's hand. He reached for Grace. Yulia sat between her parents, grinning.

Max held onto Joy, who held Tiger's hand. He grabbed Ivy's who took Darek's hand.

And his father slipped his hand into Darek's. Solid. Warm. Healthy.

Squeezed.

And the giant fist that had lived inside Darek for over a week released.

Even Sunny stuck her head up to the table, eyeing the food, her furry snout settled near his mother's hand, those brown eyes on the sandwiches.

"Let's thank God for all He's given us," his father said. "For keeping us safe in the blizzard and bringing us all home."

Darek closed his eyes, fighting the terrible burn in his throat. Yes, to all of it.

A phone buzzed and he opened his eyes to see Max pull his phone from his pocket and look at Grace. "It's the Mayo Clinic."

She drew in a breath.

He answered. "This is Max."

And when he smiled, when he turned to Grace and nodded, when he confirmed that yes, he'd be at the hospital by the New Year...

Even Darek wiped his eyes at the terrible rush of joy.

His father blew out a breath, set down his napkin. Smiled. "Let's thank the Lord for this season, this grace. The gift of Christmas."

And they did.

Because it just might be the best Christmas ever.

There was something holy about spending the night under the stars on Christmas Eve, the sky a vibrant, overwhelming display of brilliance, every star heralding the advent of the nativity.

Owen lay next to Scotty, who was quiet beside him, and wove his gloved fingers through hers. He'd shoveled them a tiny pocket of shelter at the end of the dock, making a nest for them with wool blankets. They'd bundled up in parkas, wool hats, gloves, and another blanket.

Around them, the snow covered the icy lake like a blanket of grace, and the trees creaked in the wind.

But he needed a moment, a breath alone with her.

"Are you sure this is what you want?" he asked quietly, squeezing her hand.

Scotty hadn't said much after her announcement at dinner, with most of the conversation about Max's upcoming trial, and Ivy's new appointment, and ideas for Roark and Amelia's honeymoon. And then all conversation had sort of stopped when Raina threw out a suggestion that had both shut down the conversation and somehow brought a sweet solution to a problem Owen hadn't known existed.

"What if we turned the Wilder home into a wedding venue?"

Casper had looked at her as if she'd asked him to burn the place down and rebuild it. "What—but I thought—"

"I love our little house with the drafty windows and creaky floors, Casper. It's cozy and perfect and...I don't want to leave it."

Poor guy. He'd just stared at her, no words. Until she took his face in her hands and said, "The Wilder home is beautiful. Perfect. A dream come true. And it should be shared with people looking to start their happily ever after. Like we have."

Then she'd kissed him, something sweet and chaste, but it had sort of set Casper free.

He'd spent the rest of the night grinning.

But even as Owen had sat at the table, the weight of it all swept over him.

Stay in Deep Haven.

Take over the resort.

Be a father.

Yeah, he needed a whole minute to look at the stars and just breathe.

Scotty squeezed his hand back. "I...I think so." Putting her hand on her stomach, she looked over at him.

She'd never looked so beautiful, her dark hair spilling out of a white hat, her eyes shining under the stars. "It's strange—after the wreck, something inside me just…shifted. Like I knew that life was done, and new life was starting. I just never thought it was, actually, a new life."

A new life.

Across the lake, the lights were on at Jensen Atwood's lodge, shining out on the lake. It had been over ten years since the accident that had taken Darek's first wife, the one caused by Jensen, and yet his brother had started over, taken the helm of the resort, built himself a new life.

"Owen?"

"What if…what if I screw this up?"

She rolled over, propping her head on her hand. "Screw what up?"

"It's just…big shoes to fill, you know?"

She smiled. "Owen. If anyone can fill those big shoes, it's my overachieving, driven husband."

He wanted to smile, but instead, he shook his head. "You don't understand. I think the boat accident was my fault."

Silence. A frown.

He nodded. "I was thinking about it, and I think I remember seeing rust in the rivet line—"

"Hon. The entire boat is rusty—"

"But I should have seen it."

She put her gloved hand on his cheek and turned him to face her. "It wasn't your fault any more than you losing your eye was your fault."

He met her eyes, his throat tightening. "I was reckless."

"You were a kid. You're not that kid anymore."

He nodded, but her words just couldn't settle in his heart.

"O." She sat up. "You spent your entire life watching your family live their lives while you pursued hockey. And then fishing. But in your heart, all you ever wanted was to come home."

He stared at her.

She leaned down, her face close to his. "I know you, Owen Christiansen. And God has finally given you the deepest desires of your heart."

He wrapped his arm around her, nodding, his eyes wet.

She settled in the crook of his arm, her head on his chest. "Besides, in case you're wondering, you *will* screw up."

"What?"

"You don't seriously think that you're not going to make any mistakes, right?"

"I was hoping...I guess not."

"But, Owen, that is what Christmas is about, right? The fact that we will always make mistakes, but that God fixed that. Messiah. Emmanuel." She lifted her head. "You think your faith hasn't rubbed off, but it's hard to be around a Christiansen without hearing truth and hope."

Yeah, maybe it was.

Or maybe God just wouldn't be silenced by a dark, overwhelming world.

He pulled her close, the blanket up around her shoulders.

"The strangest thing happened when I was out plowing during the blizzard. It was late, and dark, and the snow was really coming down, and all I could see was my headlights and the snow blowing off the road, and it was really blinding."

"It was a long night," she said. Indeed, he'd found her awake, staring out the window when he arrived home around five a.m.

"I pulled into the Northpoint Lodge and Truck Stop around midnight for coffee, and there was this Caravan who pulled in right behind me. Its headlights had gone out, and they'd been following the plow for an hour. I hadn't even seen them. Three guys—they were looking for a place to stay. Northpoint gave them their last room, but one of the guys joined me in the truck stop as I was fueling up, and told me that they'd been lost, parked on the side of the road after they'd nearly gotten caught in an accident, and when they saw the lights of my plow, they just started to follow it. Said it was like a miracle. He bought me coffee and a donut and even gave me a lotto ticket."

"Sounds like you saved them."

"No, the light saved them. But my dad said something before I went out to plow—remember?"

"Don't crash?"

He laughed. "No. That was you, in your head. My father told me to just follow the headlights. The thing is, the headlights only illuminate about twenty feet of road, so, all I could do was keep between the white lines and stay on the road until finally the blizzard cleared."

"And you made it home."

Yes, he'd made it home.

He looked at Scotty.

She lifted her face, smiling at him. "Merry Christmas, Owen Christiansen."

He tucked his hand under her chin and leaned in.

Yes, a very Merry Christmas, indeed.

12

"Are they still out there?"

His wife's question made John turn away from the upstairs bedroom where he'd been, yes, spying a little, on his youngest son, out on the dock with his surprising wife.

Who knew that Scotty, in the end, would be the one to save the Evergreen Resort?

Really, John had gone to the window to look at the stars, gloriously bright upon the lake. To get a final glimpse of the world he'd built. Surrendered to. Loved.

Was saying goodbye to.

Ingrid sat in their big bed, dressed in her flannel pajamas, her knees drawn up. She wore her blonde hair down, a smile on her face. Even after nearly forty years of marriage, the look in her beautiful blue eyes could still make his blood run hot in his veins, make him feel twenty-one again.

"Yes." He climbed back into the bed and drew her against him.

"Oh, the look on his face when Scotty said she was pregnant…"

"Yeah. I thought she didn't want kids," he said.

"She said that he was the one who didn't want kids. But even as she said it, I could tell... I was the one who got her the pregnancy tests."

He kissed the top of her head. "It all worked out."

"What, your master plan to get the kids home for Christmas?"

He laughed. "No. Yes. But I didn't have a plan. Just a desire. I wasn't sure how to tell them about the boat."

"I know you were worried."

"Especially after you told me about Darek and Ivy moving."

"He really had himself in a knot." She shook her head. "And that fight with Owen and Casper—I can't believe Amelia thought you were sick."

He pulled her back against himself. "I can't believe our youngest child is finally married." His fingers found their way to her hair, and he threaded them through the silkiness. "Or that Romeo actually showed up."

"He'll be a great help to Owen."

"It's time for both of them to come home."

"And for us to leave." She touched his chest, her warm hand finding his heart.

"I didn't know how God would work it out, but I knew that somehow, He would."

"Imagine that." She leaned up. "John, if there's one thing I've learned, it is that fathers know their children."

"I just hope Owen finds the life here I did."

"That's up to him. And Him."

Indeed. "So, Ingrid Young Christiansen, are you still glad you followed me to that street dance so many years ago?"

"If I remember right, you ended up in the ER."

"And you were there waiting for me."

"I just missed your smile."

He wound his arm under her neck, rolled over, cocooning her in his embrace. "Are you ready for our new adventure?"

Laughing, she hooked her fingers into the neck of his thermal shirt. "I'm going to need a promise from you."

"What promise?"

She was kissing his neck, so chances were he'd promise her anything.

"We'll always be home for Christmas," she whispered.

He lowered his mouth to hers, answered her in his kiss.

Always. But he finally drew away and met her beautiful eyes. "I promise. Because it's not Christmas unless it's at the Evergreen Resort."

The house fell silent, children dreaming, parents sleeping, their troubles out of sight.

And outside, the stars shined brightly upon a weary world as if saying, Merry Christmas to all, and to all a good night.

A NOTE FROM SUSIE MAY

Merry Christmas, my friend.

Probably one of the most common, but most under-compre-hended phrase in the human language. Merry – full of gaiety, or high spirits. Christmas—the commemoration of Christ's birth. The buoyancy of joy that comes with celebrating the advent of our Savior on earth. I feel as if this is often lost in our busy Christmas season, and especially of late, as our world struggles with the challenges of our times. We fail to stop and embrace the truth and impact of this moment.

Like so many of us, this is where the Christiansen kids find themselves. Overwhelmed. Alone. Struggling.

But, into our mess, God inserted himself, through the person of Jesus, to walk among us. So we could see the heart of God. So mankind could draw near to him as never before. So we would be saved from our sins. So we could live, and not die, forever.

This is powerful stuff and should shatter with stunning light the darkness that can sometimes feel like a cloud over our lives.

It's this truth that I hoped to write into the Christiansen Christmas. It's a truth that cuts past the clutter of our circumstances and explodes light into the dark places inside to bring hope. Promise. Joy.

Our lives can be overwhelming, but nothing—not disease, not infertility, not destroyed dreams, not a massive to-do list, not unexpected change, and not a future unknown—will separate us from God's love. Because, Emmanuel.

And that's a reason to celebrate.

Merry Christmas!

XOXO,
   Susie May

THANK YOU FOR READING

Thank you so much for reading Have Yourself a Christiansen Christmas. I hope you enjoyed the story. If you did, would you be willing to do me a favor? Head over to the product page and leave a review. It doesn't have to be long – just a few words to help other readers know what they're getting. (but no spoilers! We don't want to wreck their fun!)

I'd love to hear from you – not only about this story, but any characters or stories you'd like to read in the future. You can get ahold of me via email: susan@susanmaywarren.com.

I also have a monthly update that contains sneak peeks, reviews, upcoming releases and free, fun stuff for my reader friends. And if you'd like to see what's ahead, stop by my website at www.susanmaywarren.com

Thank you again for reading!

Susie May

ABOUT SUSAN MAY WARREN

Susan May Warren is the Christy, RITA and Carol award-winning author of over forty-five novels with Tyndale, Barbour, Steeple Hill and Summerside Press. A prolific novelist with over 1 million books sold, Susan has written contemporary and historical romances, romantic-suspense, thrillers, rom-com and Christmas novellas. She loves to help people launch their writing careers and is the founder of www.MyBookThera py.com and www.LearnHowtoWriteaNovel.com, a writing website that helps authors get published and stay published. She's also the author of the popular writing method, *The Story Equation*. Find excerpts and reviews of her novels at www. susanmaywarren.com

WHAT TO READ NEXT?

Small town Alaska. Bush pilots. Three ex-military heroes. The Kingston triplets have come home defeated, broken from war and feeling anything but heroic. But the sons of Sky King ranch have returned home just in time. Because the world is in danger, and these flyboys, rescuers and soldiers just might be the only ones who can save it. It's a fight to save the people—and country—they love, and along the way, they'll discover healing and become the heroes they are meant to be.

Wake up ladies, the Kingston brothers are back in town.

About Book 1: Sunrise

What if the woman who broke your heart was waiting for you back home...hoping for forgiveness?

Can a broken warrior find his way home to a happy ending?

After a terrible family fight, pilot Dodge Kingston left home to join the Air Force. A decade later, he's headed back to the destiny that awaits him as heir to Sky King Ranch. But that's not all that's waiting for him at home.

Echo Yazzie is a true Alaskan woman—a homesteader, dogsledder, and research guide for the DNR. After childhood best friend and former flame Dodge fled Denali, she settled into life on the Alaskan range. She's made her peace with being left behind—by her mother *and* by Dodge. And she's strong enough to live without them.

When one of Echo's fellow researchers goes missing, Echo sets out to find her, despite a blizzard, a rogue grizzly haunting the woods, and the biting cold. What she doesn't know if that, there are more than just the regular dangers of the Alaskan forests stalking her . . .

As Dodge sets out to find Echo, he can't ignore the feelings he still has for her. But will he be able to find her in time? And if he does, is there still room for him in her heart?

Learn More about Sunrise

~EXCERPT~

By the time Dodge got to the hospital, he'd already broken his first promise.

It was a Saturday, the same day the sun turned the Copper River into blades of ice, lethal and brilliant as they shoved and jockeyed out of Denali's shadow south into the Gulf of Alaska. The dawn had broken at the respectable hour of 7:42 a.m., and with it, the sunrise not only brought a southernly gust of warm air that cracked the freezing point and turned the starting line of the Iditarod to mush and grime but also laced the air with the scent of spring.

A balmy 37 degrees in Anchorage, nearly a heat wave this time of year.

Which only brought out the crazies.

As he stalked through the waiting room of Alaska Regional and punched the elevator button, Dodge shot a look at the flat-screen where the news recapped yesterday's celebration, aka the parade through Anchorage of the fifty-seven or so mushing teams. People dancing on icy berms, high-fiving the mushers, tailgaters wearing board shorts along with fur caps and mukluks, children wanting to pet the dogs. Outsiders from the Lower 48 were trying to grab selfies with local celebrities.

The mushers would be starting on their thousand-mile journey from Willow Lake later today, and with that information from the reporter, Echo Yazzie slipped into Dodge's mind.

He wondered—

No. He shook her away, got on the elevator, and rode it to the third, med-surg floor. As he got off, he recognized the smells of a hospital, not that different from Walter Reed, and his insides clenched.

He wouldn't stay long.

Of course, the old man hadn't died in the accident, and maybe that was crass of Dodge, but if he had, maybe it would all be over, the burn in Dodge's gut finally extinguished.

He spotted his sister, Larke, standing at the end of the hall, staring through the window at the blue sky, the muddy streets. She stood with her back to him, so he only guessed it was Larke, her long blonde hair in a singular braid down her back. But she also wore a Sky King Ranch flight jacket, the words emblazoned on the back, so that seemed a dead giveaway.

A man sat in a nearby molded chair, his hair cut military short. He considered Larke with worried eyes.

Probably Riley McCord, her SEAL husband. *Perfect.* With Dodge's luck, his brother Range and Riley would have met on some classified SEAL mission, become best of pals, and Riley would have gotten an earful of family dirty laundry over a post-mission debriefing.

Dodge, of course, starring as the villain of the story.

He braced himself. "Larke?"

She turned, and of course she looked older—the last time he'd seen her she'd been eighteen and joining the Army.

And he'd been sixteen and just stupid enough to think that he had his life buttoned up.

"Dodge?" She wore trauma in her eyes, probably fatigue and

worry, but also residue from the years she'd served as a medic. Still, he wondered if she had been the one to find the wreckage of their father's DHC-3 Otter bush plane. His friend Moose had been sketchy on that part when he'd called to tell Dodge about the accident.

Glancing at the man in the chair, who rose, Larke put her coffee on the ledge of the window. "Wow. I didn't think . . . I mean . . . how did you find out?"

Dodge wished she'd finished her first thought. She didn't think . . . *what?* That he cared about the old man? That he'd ever return? That he didn't think about his choices nearly every day, especially recently?

"Moose Mulligan, down at Air One Rescue," Dodge answered.

Larke wore a pair of jeans, Sorels, and a wedding ring on her left hand, but he knew that, too, thanks to the *Copper Mountain Good News*'s online portal.

He just kept his subscription for the obits. And maybe the police report. Really. The fact that it listed her engagement to a Navy SEAL a couple years ago was just a bonus line item.

"Have you been in Anchorage all this time?" She seemed to be working her words, trying not to accuse.

He felt it anyway.

"How'd it happen?" He glanced at the other man—Riley— now standing. Big enough, built like a linebacker, he stepped close to Larke and put his arm around her.

Dodge met his eyes even as Larke spoke.

"Otto Smith saw him go down and called it in. Dad was low, coming in for a landing at the Copper Mountain airfield, and his wing clipped a tree. Otto wasn't sure but he thought the wing might have detached before it hit."

"A faulty wing attachment?" His gaze went back to Larke, having found some solid ground in his silent face-off with Riley. Riley loved her—he would protect her, and Dodge appreciated that. Larke might be two years older than him, but she was still his sister.

"It's the only way we can figure it." Her gaze flitted toward the closed door that Dodge guessed was the old man's room. "He's been flying for forty-nine years. He doesn't make mistakes."

"It doesn't have to be a pilot error for accidents to happen, Larke. Weather. A wind gust. Anything can happen in the bush."

Her jaw clenched and her husband tightened his grip on her. He finally held out his hand to Dodge. "Riley McCord."

Dodge met it. "Dodge Kingston. When did you two finally hitch up?"

"Before my first tour," he said. "About a year ago."

Dodge didn't ask if he knew Ranger, figured it would come up if it needed to. "Congrats. Sorry I wasn't there."

"We eloped," Larke said. "You and the boys were too hard to track down, and Dad already gave his blessing, so . . ."

She was being kind with her words. Truth was, he hadn't a clue where Ranger, and especially Colt, had landed on the globe. And he didn't ask. Just because they were triplets didn't mean they were close. At least, not anymore.

"How bad is it?" He gestured with his head toward door number one.

"Dislocated shoulder, broken arm, a couple cracked ribs. One of them nicked his lung, though, and it collapsed. Moose and a team from Air One Rescue flew in to the crash site. Took them forever, but they did save his life." She frowned. "But you know that. What, are you flying for them now?"

Dodge wrapped a hand around the back of his neck. Not really. Maybe. "Moose has my number and he called me."

He left out the part where he'd gotten on a plane in DC and flown eight-plus hours before he'd let his brain kick in.

It wasn't like his father wanted him around. Or like Dodge

would swoop in and save the ranch, walk back into the life he'd longed for once upon a time.

Pick up where he left off with the girl he left behind.

Clearly, he needed a shower, breakfast, and coffee—although he'd given up the last one during his stint in Walter Reed, so maybe just tea. He'd promised his docs to keep his heart rate at a reasonable tick going forward.

Still, maybe he needed to offer Larke something of an explanation because she just looked at him, through him, clearly not believing him. But if he kept going with his explanation there'd be more judgment, questions, and who knew. He'd end up doing something he swore he'd never do.

Like return home.

Nope. His stupid impulses had done enough damage. "How long are you in town?"

"We've been here about ten days. Riley has about a week left on leave." She wrapped her arms around herself. "I should have gone with Dad."

"Larke," Riley said quietly, "he's been flying by himself for years."

Maybe he didn't mean the indictment, but Dodge's chest tightened anyway.

She glanced at Riley. "What? I know what I'm doing up there."

A muscle ticked in Riley's jaw.

Behind them, the door opened, and Dodge turned just as a doctor in her midforties walked out. She seemed no-nonsense, with short brown hair, seasoned eyes, and a lean frame. She wore a jacket over a pair of scrubs and held out her hand to Larke.

"I'm Doctor Madison. I operated on your father. He's going to be pretty sore, and we're going to keep him here for another day or two, but he's a tough one. He'll be okay."

Dodge's throat thickened with her words.

"Thanks, Doc," Larke said for them both. "Can we see him?"

Doc Madison nodded, and Larke headed for the door.

Dodge didn't move.

Larke stopped, turned. "Really?"

"It's been ten years, Larke. I know you weren't around, but . . . it was bad. He doesn't want to see me."

Her mouth tightened around the edges. "Don't be stupid. You're here. Come in with me."

He held up his hand. "He's wounded. Maybe now's not the time to—"

"See his oldest son? Confirm that you're not dead in some Taliban-occupied valley in Afghanistan? Yeah, you're probably right. He wouldn't want to know that you're okay and standing in the hallway afraid to walk in and say hi to your father."

Oh, she could light him up. He clenched his jaw.

Riley looked away and shoved his hands in his pockets.

"What are you afraid of, Dodge?"

"I'm not afraid, Larke."

She met his gaze, and in hers he saw a woman who'd been through her own trauma and survived. So not the girl who needed to be protected, not anymore.

Fine. "I left for a reason, and that reason hasn't changed."

"Hasn't it?"

A beat passed, and he didn't move.

She opened the door and went inside.

Riley gave him a thin-lipped smile and followed.

Dodge walked to the end of the hallway and stared out the window.

With the break in the freeze, blackened snowdrifts edged the parking lot, muddy with thawing rivers of ice. Cars splashed mud, and ice floated in the Knik Arm waterway. The view looked out over Merrill Airfield and the hundred or so parked Beavers, Otters, Cessnas, and Piper Cubs that roamed the skies, then extended past the airfield to Joint Base Elmendorf-

Richardson, to the north. Beyond it, the ridge back of the Alaskan range razored across the sun-soaked blue sky, bold and white and impressive. Denali and Huntington, Foraker and Russell, were tucked in there, each glacial runnel and granite ridge imprinted in him like the lines of his palm.

The mountains called to him like an old familiar song, a tune embedded in his bones.

One he was trying to forget.

Though he couldn't see it from here, Sky King Ranch was nestled in the foothills of the range, perched on a lake that hosted cabins and a lodge for the family.

They also ran thirty or so head of cattle and a handful of horses.

Barry Kingston, his father, was one of few remaining born and bred Alaskans in Copper Mountain. And his sons were supposed to carry on the legacy.

Dodge crossed his arms akimbo, glued there because, of course, Larke was right.

He *was* afraid. Afraid of the memories that still broke free sometimes. And most of all, afraid of the words that he longed to hear and never would.

He should leave. He'd made himself promises, and he'd already broken the first one by standing in this corridor. Stupid instincts.

"Oh, thank God, Dodge, you're here."

The voice jolted him, made him turn.

Winter Starr. Daughter of the legendary bush pilot Sheldon Starr. Her family ran Starr Air Service, northwest of Copper Mountain. She wore her dark hair in two long braids and had on a pair of boots and a Starr Air sweatshirt. She probably ran her own plane by now.

He had no words when she walked right up to him and pulled him down in a hug. "I'm so sorry about your dad."

She'd beat him out for valedictorian by a half point and that had intrigued, if not irked, him enough to like her. But she'd also been Echo's best friend, so that was as far as his interest went.

"Thanks."

She let him go. "I was coming up to talk to Larke, but I'm so glad you're here. We can divvy up his charters, but I can't do his mail route, Dodge. I just can't."

He raised an eyebrow.

"I've already got the mail run to Paxton, plus every homestead east of the Copper River, and if I add the western mail, that fills me right up."

"You're running the mail?"

"And medical and groceries for most of the east side north of Susitna. Your dad has the western run, over the range, to Nikolai and Stony River, and even out to Russian Mission."

Of course he did. An area that would probably keep him in the air for days.

"He also checks in on the homesteads in the area—he's got a schedule."

"I know it." He'd flown that route more times than he could count.

She cut her voice down. "They're talking pilot error."

"No. Otto Smith said his wing was coming off."

"Ernie Wright just did a hundred-hour inspection on the plane. It was cleared." She sighed. "I don't know how much you know, but your dad has had a few close calls lately. Nearly clipped another plane in the Copper Mountain airfield during taxi, and I heard he spooked a recent group by flying too close to one of Huntington Mountain's spires."

"Aw, that's just Barry Kingston showing off."

"The National Air Transportation Board is coming in to do an investigation, and depending on what they find, he could be shut down. At the very least, he can't fly, not for a while, right?" She gestured to his room.

"Larke is here. She knows the routes—"

"In her condition? I'm surprised that Riley let her get in a plane with me to fly them down."

Condition? So that's what the look between them was about.

Winter's expression portrayed concern. "I get it—high-risk pregnancy and all that, but he's a little overprotective, if you ask me. But that's a SEAL for you." Her voice turned sweet. "Where've you been, anyway? Someone said Air Force."

"Something like that."

"Afghanistan?"

"Sometimes."

"I heard your brothers are big shot military guys too. Ranger made the SEALs."

Dodge nodded.

"And Colt, some sort of special forces in the Army?"

Delta Force, according to Ranger. Dodge lifted a shoulder.

"All a bunch of overachieving heroes, aren't you?" Her eyes shone, maybe a little of their untried past in them. "Glad you're back."

"I'm not back," he said, the words just slipping out.

Winter frowned.

And what was he going to say? That not only had he vowed to never return to Sky King Ranch but he wasn't keen on getting in the cockpit again either?

He shouldn't be here, for so many reasons. But Winter was the last person who should know that. Mostly because if Winter knew, then her sister Shasta knew . . . and if Shasta knew, well it wouldn't take long for the entire town to buzz with the news.

So he found a benign smile. "Never mind. Good to see you, Winter."

"Your dad keeps that yellow Piper 14 you used to fly tuned up. I saw him out in it a few weeks back. You flew that thing like it was a part of you. Like you had wings."

He'd forgotten that. But yes, she was right. Once upon a

time, the sky felt like home. Maybe it would again—he just had to get back on the proverbial horse-slash-cockpit.

Or not.

"Well, like I said, I'm glad you're back." She looked at him, paused. Then, "She will be too."

His smile faded. "I didn't ask."

"Sure you did." She winked and walked away, and his heart slammed like a fist in his chest.

"She will be too."

The door to the room opened and Riley stepped out. "Going for more coffee. Your dad is still sleeping. Larke didn't get much sleep last night."

He didn't move down the hall, however, and again Dodge braced himself.

"Listen," Riley said. "I don't know what went down, and she doesn't talk about it, but she can't stay, Dodge." He took a breath, looked past Dodge to the window, his mouth tightening. "She lost our first baby about six months ago, so this one is higher risk. I can't have her up there, doing . . . well, I'm well aware of the perils of being a bush pilot." He shook his head. "We met the summer of the Copper Mountain fire. The one that took out your grandparents' house. She was a daredevil, even then. I can't—"

Dodge held up his hand. "Stop. I get it."

Riley turned his gaze on him. "Get this, then. If you don't fly, he loses his contracts. And if he loses his contracts—"

"He could lose the ranch. I can do the math, Riley. Once upon a time, I was planning on taking over Sky King Ranch."

Silence fell between them.

"You weren't planning on going home, were you?" Riley asked.

Maybe the guy was an interrogator, but Dodge had no secrets, not really.

The entire town knew why he'd left. He shook his head.

"Why are you in town?" Riley asked.

What could it hurt? "I have a job offer with Air One Rescue flying choppers." He'd been sitting on his answer for a while now, not sure of the wisdom of saying yes to a job that might be doomed, but what else could he do?

His answer seemed made when Moose called him.

"I see. So nearby, but not all the way home." Riley raised an eyebrow.

"You should stop right there, because you don't know anything about it."

"I know that I wish, with everything inside me, that I had a second chance to show my pop that I turned out okay. That I finally became the person he knew I could be."

"My father couldn't care less how I turned out." And that came out exactly as bitter as it tasted in his chest.

"He has your picture on his mantel," Riley said.

"He probably has my brothers' pictures up there too."

Riley nodded slowly.

Dodge drew in a breath. Managed not to put his fist in the wall. Instead, he sighed and said, "Okay, here's the bottom line. Nothing has changed since the day I walked into the recruiter's office and enlisted. I'm not back. I'll fly his routes until he can take over, but you tell Larke not to mistake any of this for a happy ending. There's no sunrise of hope here." He glanced out the window at the slush and rivers of melting snow. "This winter isn't over, and everyone should just calm down. We have at least one more deadly blizzard ahead of us."

Riley gave a slow nod. "Okay. So how do you like your coffee?"

Dodge looked at him. Right. So much for promises. "Black and bracing."

Get your copy of Sunrise, in stores now!

Have Yourself A Christiansen Christmas

Published by SDG Publishing

Copyright © 2021 by Susan May Warren

Ebook ISBN: 978-1-943935-53-6

Print ISBN: 978-1-943935-54-3

Hardback ISBN: 978-1-943935-55-0

Scripture quotations are taken from the King James Version of the Bible.

Scripture quotations are also taken from the Holy Bible, New International Version®, NIV®. Copyright© 1973, 1978, 1984, 2011 by Biblica, Inc®. Used by permission of Zondervan. All rights reserved worldwide.

For more information about Susan May Warren, please access the author's website at the following address: www.susanmaywarren.com.

Published in the United States of America.

Made in the USA
Middletown, DE
03 December 2023

44503107R00138